I0762136

BURNT

A NOVEL

GENE UPCHURCH

This is a work of fiction. Names, characters, places, and incidents either are the product of the author's imagination or are used fictitiously. Any resemblance to actual persons, living or dead, events, or locales is entirely coincidental.

Firebrand Publishing publishes in a variety of print and electronic formats and by print-on-demand. For more information about Firebrand Publishing products, visit https://firebrandpublishing.com

ISBN 978-1-941907-56-6 (*hardcover*)

ISBN 978-1-941907-55-9 (*eBook*)

Published by Firebrand Publishing

Printed in the United States of America

CONTENTS

For the kids in my life:

Mav, Zoe, Henry & Caroline

The characters in this book are not your role models

"Y'all play with fire,
y'all gonna get burnt."

Warning from mommas everywhere

I. THE HOUSE

The house had to go.

That's why he was here.

He crouched in the chilly darkness. It was winter, and the owner had turned down the heat because no one was there for weeks or months.

The wind from the north buffeted the two-million-dollar house, perched on one of the island's best dunes, a prime spot at the confluence of the river and the ocean, a great spot to watch ships enter the river and to savor magnificent sunsets as they bring satisfying conclusions to happy beach days.

But tonight, the house moaned as the wind blew against it. It was a sad, low sigh of a moan, as if the house knew it was loved no more, that it was doomed, and excited voices would never be heard here again.

Jeff had come from the mainland on a fifteen-foot skiff, lights out, the sound of the small outboard motor blown out to sea by the persistent wind. He puttered down the river and stayed as close to the mainland shore as he could, hoping no one would see him. He paused briefly to allow a huge container ship to pass, its massive engines a soft rumble in the night. In its wake was the pilot boat, following along to retrieve the local river pilot who knew the mysteries of the complex and ever-shifting shoals and sandbars and other hazards and whose job was to help a captain from the other side of the world avoid them.

About a minute after the massive ship passed, Jeff maneuvered his tiny craft to point its bow toward the spot in the river where the ship had just been. A less experienced sailor than Jeff would not know that the wake from a massive ship, even a slow-moving ship, is like an ocean wave, and would easily capsize a tiny boat like Jeff's, especially if you're caught unaware in the dark. But Jeff knew better, and the large wake passed under his boat without damage.

As he got his boat back on course, Jeff wondered if the powerful radars on the ship and pilot boat would pick him up, and eventually betray him, but it was unlikely they would. The ship's radar was focused on finding obstacles on the horizon, and the pilot boat didn't care about crazy fishermen out at this time of night.

When the ship and pilot boat moved on, Jeff resumed his dark trip down the river, finally into the ocean and into an abrupt crosswind, the waves threatening to overturn his tiny craft. He ran the boat up on the beach about fifty yards from the big house and pulled out the Igloo cooler that contained his supplies.

The house had an alarm, but Jeff knew it was off tonight. It was easy to break into the house, and he quickly moved around and placed eight tiny homemade bombs in strategic places around it.

And now he crouched and thought for a moment, knowing the chaos and drama that would follow his next moves.

He sipped a cold beer that he purloined from the beach house fridge. He looked around the beautiful home which had only minutes to live and, even though it was dark, he could see it was a fabulous place. He cared nothing for the reasons why people wanted to burn down their stuff, especially stuff they loved, but he knew it was almost always about the money.

He waited weeks for a night like tonight, when a steady and predictable wind blew from the north. The wind would blow the smoke and sparks and ashes out into the sea rather than back onto the island, and no one would smell the smoke, delaying a response that would help him escape and ensure the death of the house.

He went to his first little homemade bomb. It was under the front porch, where the owner stored electric golf carts, fishing poles, beach bikes and boogie boards, all the tools of happy beach vacations. He set the bomb's timer; each subsequent timer was set a little shorter. If he calculated correctly, they'd all ignite at nearly the same time.

As he twisted the timer on the last bomb, the first one under the porch ignited with a pop. He immediately smelled the burning fuel and could see flames outside. The others popped in quick succession; he counted eight pops and saw small flames everywhere. He opened the double doors on the beach deck and quickly moved across the house to open the door facing the island. The wind charged into the house, almost angrily, whipping the small flames into something lethal.

He surveyed his work as the flames grew more serious and the house filled with smoke. It was a strange sensation to go from total darkness to a house filled with a flickering, deadly light.

He took a final slug of beer and left the house. He trotted across the beach to his tiny boat, pushed it into the water, and climbed in. He could see far out in the ocean that the pilot boat had completed its task and was fighting the head wind, bobbing up and down as it made the tedious run back to its base. He wondered if they would see the fire.

But the first call came into the tiny island fire department from the Coast Guard station across the river. A house fire on your island, a big one, fully engaged.

The island fire department was excellent, but its two firefighters on duty this winter night would be no match for the inferno. The firefighters had no address, but they saw the blaze as soon as they turned onto the beach road and immediately radioed the mainland for more trucks and manpower.

That help would arrive by barge in an hour, perhaps. The barge captain was awakened and arrived at the dock as quickly as he could where he found waiting for him three fire engines from three different communities, a brush truck from a fourth, and a tanker from yet another. He was momentarily emotional about the show of support, but he knew these firefighters loved the action and were excited to help. He carefully organized the loading of the fire trucks on the barge to ensure all the weight was equally balanced.

The trip to the island usually took about forty-five minutes, but the captain pushed his limits to nearly twelve knots to shear a few minutes off the voyage. For reasons he didn't understand, the firefighters kept the red lights flashing on their trucks, so it was quite a spectacle as the barge moved down the river and turned toward the orange glow of the big fire on the horizon. A crowd gathered on the river's edge to cheer them on and capture the moment on their phones.

Other firefighters arrived by boat, some on their personal boats, others on boats owned by their fire department. Some of the boats docked at the marina, and the firefighters walked from there or caught a ride with islanders who wanted to help. Others piloted their boats right to the beach in front of the conflagration and crossed the dunes to go to work.

There also was an antique fire boat docked up the river, and its water cannon could reach the house if they could find the boat's old drunk captain, but they never did, and it wouldn't have helped anyway.

While waiting for reinforcements from the mainland, plenty of island folk rushed to the scene to help. Some were trained volunteer firemen, and some just wanted to be a part of the action, grateful it wasn't their house.

None of this mattered. Ashes and sparks and pieces of wood and fabric from the beautiful house fell into the ocean, their steamy hisses as they hit the cold water disguised by the constant sound of the surf. Explosions erupted as propane tanks for the gas grill and batteries for the golf cars overheated. Heavy smoke sailed southward toward the Coast Guardsmen, who could smell it even from a distance as they watched through their binoculars as the house burned down.

Amidst the smoke and flames and drama and the darkness of the winter night, no one noticed the skiff, just offshore, chugging toward the river.

The local newspaper ran a smartphone photo of the house fully engulfed, and the big fire set tongues wagging all over the island. Lightning? A golf cart charger overheated? Insurance fraud? The county fire investigator figured the fire started under the porch near the golf carts, and the house was so thoroughly destroyed that he spent no more time trying to figure out what happened.

As required by local ordinances, the owner's insurance company paid a demolition crew to bulldoze the site within thirty days.

When they left, it was as if the house never existed.

II. THE RIVER

Nobody knew his name, and he didn't advertise on the hundreds of billboards that lined the beach road, but Jeff was the coastal community's arsonist of choice.

He pretty much ran a monopoly. He was a professional who could be trusted to burn your house, barn, car, boat, or business and do it so thoroughly and efficiently that it always looked like an act of God or an unfortunate accident.

If you needed the service he provided, you talked to a guy who knew a guy and dropped the cash and the plans at the Crazy Crab, a dark and smelly beer joint that served the local drunks who were always there and boaters who stopped at the marina on their way to somewhere else.

His homemade bombs were a simple design that exploded reliably and burned so intensely that it was nearly impossible for the county's harried fire inspector to ever detect something amiss when he crawled through the sooty wreckage of a rental house that needed too many expensive repairs or poked through the charred leftovers of a luxury car whose transmission was slipping and its owner had done the math and it was cheaper to burn than fix.

He had perfected his little bombs and timers in the dark woods near his trailer on the mainland. They were so volatile that his tests in the woods threatened to start a major forest fire every time.

The secret in his secret sauce was Jet A aviation fuel. He had a source at the little airport on the mainland who would sell it to him for five hundred dollars a gallon, which was obviously a total rip off. His source didn't know what he needed with aviation fuel, but he knew it wasn't for an airplane so Jeff was satisfied with the arrangement because five hundred bucks would buy a lot of silence. He used the jet fuel because it burned cleaner and hotter and didn't leave behind the smell of gasoline to tip off investigators that an accelerant had been used.

He used old Gatorade bottles because they were just the right size, and their plastic was just the right consistency to completely melt and leave no trace. He linked the timers to old-fashioned M80 firecrackers that he bought just over the border in South Carolina where they're legal. When the M80s popped, they ignited the jet fuel in the bottle, and then it was on.

He called them his "gator bombs."

Jeff's specialty was boats. There were thousands in the area, tucked into marinas up and down the intracoastal waterway. Nearly all were more than their owners could afford to own, and there was always somebody who fell behind on payments or lost the boat in a divorce or just decided that a boat was more trouble than it was worth.

He blew up dozens of boats up and down the coast and made everybody think that diesel or gas fumes had built up in the engine compartment, and an innocent spark had ignited a calamity. He found it useful to have a secondary method for sinking boats so that every floating casualty in the area didn't have the same look or feel. His other tactic wasn't technically "arson." His little bombs could blow out the bottom of a boat right next to the transom, quickly sinking the doomed vessel right where it was moored. He, of course, always loosened the mooring lines at the dock so they wouldn't prevent the boat from sinking.

He only did about a job a month. Any more than that would be a "rash of arsons" and draw unneeded attention. He had amassed nearly a hundred thousand dollars, all in a hidden place in the woods near his trailer. He spent very little of it, relying on the income from his maintenance job at the Hampton Inn out on the highway to support his modest lifestyle. The hidden cash was his retirement fund.

Then, one day, there was a suspicious fire. It wasn't his. An old barn was torched on the outskirts of town, and a woman was badly injured rescuing three horses that were stabled inside. It was a sloppy arson; it was obviously set by an amateur, and the county fire investigator was on full alert.

Jeff was concerned and puzzled. He was proud of his craft, and also proud that he had standards that ensured no person or animal was ever injured on one of his jobs. He always made a special point to confirm that nobody was hooked up below decks with a girlfriend or boyfriend before he blew up their love nest.

A week later, another apparent arson, this time an abandoned convenience store that had fallen into disrepair and didn't meet county code anymore. The word around town is that you could smell the gasoline from blocks away. Amateur.

Was somebody moving in on his business? If so, their sloppy approach and frequent fires were a threat to him. He didn't want anybody thinking that's how he did business, but it wasn't possible to take out an ad in the local newspaper or run a radio commercial explaining this to the public.

It was now clear to him: somebody was moving in, and they were sloppy.

And the only way to fight fire, he reckoned, is with fire.

Jeff spent several weeks poking around town quietly, patiently, and cleverly. The bartender at the Crazy Crab was helpful; a lot of folks confided in him, some of them more than they should.

Jeff finally found a guy who knew the guy who was the front man for the new arsonist.

And on this night, he hid in the woods where he had a clear view of his own narrow driveway and the little clearing where his trailer sat. His truck was hidden nearby, where a careless arsonist wouldn't see it.

He had set a trap, and his poor little trailer was the bait.

If his plan went well, the town would have only a single arsonist in a few hours.

Jeff had worked with the bartender at the Crazy Crab and another guy to lure in the new arsonist with the promise of a couple of lucrative jobs. But first, there was a job to torch a trailer out in the country, Jeff's trailer, and Jeff would be waiting.

Headlights turned off the main road and lit up the two tracks in the driveway that cut through the scrub pines that shielded his home from the main road. An old Jeep entered the clearing and stopped. The driver flicked on the high beams and pointed the Jeep at the trailer to light it up.

Two people emerged from the Jeep. Jeff hadn't planned on that. He figured all arsonists were like him, lone wolves, sole proprietors.

He stared at them. High school kids, giggling as they shared a joint and checked out his trailer. Jeff thought, *this will be easier than I expected.*

It was clear they were stoned out of their minds. They leaned on the hood of the Jeep as they finished the joint, then weaved around, laughing and acting brave with their hands on their hips, unsteady as they surveyed Jeff's trailer and tried to decide their next move. When they talked, Jeff could hear their conversation, and they sounded like the California stoners you see in the movies.

Jeff slowly walked from the dark woods. He crept closer and got to about ten feet from the pair. He flipped on his big flashlight and held it beneath his chin.

Boo.

The driver whipped around in shock, and his partner shrieked, waving his arms up and down like a frightened girl.

"Let's get out of here!," screamed the driver as he scrambled wildly back to the Jeep, joined by his colleague who bounced off the Jeep's fender and fell on the gravel in his panic to get back in it.

Jeff couldn't reach them before they threw the Jeep in reverse, the truck's big tires flinging rocks and dirt as they escaped down his driveway and almost wrecked as they turned onto the road in front of Jeff's trailer.

Jeff sprinted to his hidden truck and tried to follow their taillights, but they had quickly rushed down the road. He caught up enough to see them turn onto the lane that led down to the river where a little cove and a small dock served the neighborhood's sailors and their boats. There was only one small light dimly illuminating the dock; most of these sailors didn't venture out at night.

When Jeff slid to a halt at the end of the lane, he saw the Jeep had been parked clumsily or wrecked, with the right front tire in a ditch and the left rear in the air and still spinning helplessly. He saw the two miscreants frantically going to each of the eight or so boats moored at the dock, clearly looking in desperation for a boat whose owner had left the keys in the switch.

"Here's one!" shouted the driver as he jumped in the nice 35-foot Grady White and cranked its twin outboards as his buddy quickly untied her.

The driver pushed the throttles to the max and wildly spun the wheel. The boat hit the dock with a glancing blow, putting a nasty scrape in the hull and nearly tossing the two potheads into the cove as they laughed and flipped the bird at Jeff. The boat jumped so abruptly that it nearly smashed into an adjacent boat before it made a U-turn, roared out of the little cove, and quickly disappeared into the darkness.

I can't let these losers get away, Jeff thought. *The cops can find them by tracking the Jeep's tags, but they didn't really commit a crime tonight until they stole the boat, except for maybe trespassing. The Jeep might be stolen, also. Not much to go on. I need to follow them, at least get an idea of where they're going.*

A buddy of Jeff's kept a small fishing boat at the dock, and Jeff had been with him and seen where he hid the key. It would never keep up with the Grady White, but maybe he could see where they went.

He entered the river, but it was dark and a marine layer had settled, a thick fog that occurs when warm air passes over the cold water. If he looked straight up, he could see the stars. Looking straight ahead, he could see nothing. He slowed, and could hear the Grady White, its engines shrieking in the darkness.

The enormous container ship barely fit into the channel where the river flowed into the sea. At the helm was a Norwegian captain who was weary from a stormy trip up the east coast after traversing the Panama Canal.

At his side on the bridge was a seasoned local river pilot who had grown up on the river and knew and understood its personality. He had joined the ship about twenty miles from the river's entrance after a bumpy ride on the pilot boat.

The darkness of the night and the foggy marine layer made it impossible to navigate without the ship's modern GPS system.

Its three spinning radars outlined the river channel and all its buoys to give the team on the bridge a clear picture of what lie ahead. Otherwise, they were blind. There was no point in looking out the windows of the bridge. The fog was so thick that they couldn't even see the ship's bow light.

Once they made a couple of complex turns entering the river, the container ship had an easy fifteen-mile run up the river to the port where the captain could finally rest, and his crew could get drunk.

It was late, so there was little traffic on the river. The captain and pilot watched blue dots on the powerful radars as the island passenger ferry made its hourly run and passed on the port side, and the state-owned river auto ferry passed to their stern. The captain and pilot watched the blue dots steadily move away.

In spite of the fog, the crew on the bridge began to see the orange lights of the port warm the clouds in the dark sky miles ahead of them. The pilot quietly issued navigational orders to the captain and his helmsman, and the ship chugged northward.

The captain and pilot were drinking coffee and chatting when the spinning radars picked up a blue dot off the port bow, two miles and closing. The helmsman watched the radar, and when the dot failed to adjust its course to avoid the ship, he called to his captain.

The Norwegian and the pilot watched the radar as the blue dot headed straight for them. The pilot jogged to the port side flying bridge to look with his own eyes, but could see nothing in the darkness and fog, and returned to the radar.

The blue dot was now a mile out and closing. The captain

and pilot looked at each other and knew what had to be done. The captain ordered his ship to a full stop, but that might take a half a mile, and all lights to be illuminated. Collision alarms rang, and the ship's bow lights lit up the river. He sounded the ship's enormous foghorn, three long blasts that were heard throughout the county.

Still, the blue dot came, a thousand yards, five hundred yards, no sign of turning. Three more long blasts.

The captain and pilot stepped quickly to the port flying bridge, where they could see the entire length of the ship. The blue dot on the radar emerged from the fog to become a gleaming white pleasure boat, still speeding directly at them, bouncing in the river's small swales, enormous spray from the boat's bow. Surely, the Grady White could see them now that all the lights were on.

They watched helplessly as the boat's operator wildly flailed at the wheel, but not reduce its speed. The boat nearly capsized as it violently turned, not away from the ship but towards it, and they could see its occupants falling and rolling around in the boat. The boat was out of control.

One of the boat's occupants flailed wildly as he fell into the river just as the 35-footer crashed into the side of the container ship about 100 feet from the port bow, a quick pop of flame at the waterline as the Grady White's gas tank ruptured. The captain and pilot on the flying bridge felt nothing, but they saw the sickening remains of craft being sucked under the ship in its powerful vortex and another man overboard, not moving.

The big ship was still moving, so the captain ordered the engines reversed to stop the ship more quickly, sounded the ship's alarms, sent a rescue team into the river, and asked for a damage assessment to the ship's hull. The pilot sent a distress signal to the local coast guard station.

Jeff was a mile or more away when it happened, chugging through the fog and darkness in the little fishing boat, squinting, trying to see anything at all. He might as well have had a bag over his head. He heard what he thought was the soothing low rumble of a big ship, and the sound of the Grady White's engines in the distance.

He was startled, however, when the river suddenly became alive. There was a glow in the fog as the lights of a huge ship came on and, a few seconds later, the booming sound of its horn, impossible to miss.

Jeff couldn't see through the fog, but he could still hear the Grady White's engines until there was a metallic clank, a momentary bright light, and the sound of the engines stopped. The ship's alarms sounded.

He stood in the fishing boat, hand over his mouth, speechless.

Those poor idiots, he thought.

Jeff returned to the tiny cove with the borrowed fishing boat and got back in his truck. He heard sirens, very close by, and drove as quickly as he could toward his trailer.

His home was in flames. Two fire trucks were in the clearing, pouring water and trying to keep it from spreading into the woods.

He found the fire captain and told him it was his home. The captain said he was sorry and told him it was clear the trailer had been torched. The captain waved over a sheriff's deputy.

The deputy said he was sorry, also, but we caught the guy who did it.

Jeff's mind went blank.

"Yep," the deputy said, "caught him leaving your driveway, and he smelled like gas. We were looking for kids who were stealing Amazon boxes from people's porches, so we got lucky. He's confessed to some other fires. I'm sorry we couldn't do more to save your house, but it went real quick."

The fire chief walked over to Jeff.

"I gotta go, but my guys will stay here until everything's safe," he said. "Bad boat wreck in the river. Coast Guard and our river rescue just got dispatched. Apparently, a motorboat just hit a cargo ship. Sounds bad."

Jeff couldn't think straight.

Those poor, stupid kids, nothing more than petty thieves, too stoned to operate a boat in the pitch-black darkness, running from me. Why did I chase them?

While the fire crews focused on his trailer, he slipped into the woods and sat on his haunches, stunned by everything that was happening. He had caused this entire mess, the fire, what sounds like a horrible wreck in the river. He took a deep, cleansing breath to stifle a sob that was building.

This is not who I am, but look at the pain I caused, he thought. *I should've left those kids alone, but I thought they were gonna burn down my trailer.*

He sat in the dark, damp woods.

The only sounds were the crackling of the remaining flames and the calm voices of the firefighters finishing up their jobs.

III. THE COASTIE

Three years earlier, the sound he heard was of a heavy wooden gavel falling at the conclusion of his trial, and five commanders in the US Coast Guard looked down at Jeff from their lofty and imposing bench, their brows furrowed. Jeff's head was bowed, staring at the green and white linoleum floor of the courtroom of the Judge Advocate General, so he could not see the sadness and frustration on all their faces.

Jeff couldn't believe it was ending this way, an end to the only two things he had ever wanted and had ever loved.

When Jeff graduated after an aimless high school experience, he knew what he wanted to do. He had always loved boats and was lucky to have a dad and some uncles who also loved boats and were excellent skippers. He learned from them and figured the best way to have a job that was fun was to be a "coastie."

The Coast Guard was happy to have him, because he

already had knowledge of boats and how to operate one. He passed all the tests and breezed through basic training, and was assigned to a patrol boat near Brunswick, Georgia. He started as a simple sailor, but he learned everything about the boat and its safe and responsible operation and got a real kick and genuine pleasure from the crew's work to help people and save many of them from the idiocy of the so-called captains of their boats.

Boats overturned, boats ran out of gas, boats hit other boats, boats ran aground, and sometimes they caught fire and sank for no apparent reason. Sometimes people got hurt, and sometimes the so-called captains got arrested because they were too drunk to know starboard from port. Sometimes they were running drugs, and then it was a different story. Once they were smuggling human beings, an experience he never forgot, because he was truly helping to save helpless lives.

Jeff loved every minute of it and paid special attention to the process of investigating the incidents, and the careful attention to the smallest detail that usually enabled the investigators to zero in on what happened. He watched and learned how to dissect a crash or a fire and ask the right questions of the people who often were flung overboard, or who clung to a floating ice chest after their vessel had sunk to the bottom.

He was promoted quickly to helmsman, so he got to operate the powerful patrol boat, even though the commander was in charge and told him where to go.

This was the most fun he'd ever had, and most days he found it hard to believe his good fortune. The commander was a cool guy, so he never minded if Jeff roared into a small marina with great fanfare, ignoring the no-wake signs, and swirling the noisy boat with its machine gun mounted on the bow around in a couple of big loops, catching the attention of everyone.

From the docks, it looked like the Coast Guard was after a drug dealer or a human smuggler, when the sailors were actually using their powerful binoculars to look at girls.

They rarely docked on these visits, just pirouetted the powerful boat around a couple of times and then roar off. Occasionally, Jeff would steer the boat into a small marina, and the commander would call out to the crew, "Code White!" Everyone but Jeff seemed to know what this meant, but to Jeff it meant pulling the boat to the most convenient mooring spot and tying her up, leaving her engines idling while his crewmates and the commander jumped off and sauntered to the dockmaster's office or whatever little store served whatever marina they were in.

On this particular day, it was blistering hot. There is no air conditioning in the bridge of a patrol boat, so keeping the boat moving and circulating a little breeze was essential to fight the heat.

As they roared into a little island marina, the commander called out "Code White," and Jeff slowed the boat and maneuvered toward the fuel dock where all the spaces were occupied by little fishing boats. There was no spot for the coasties.

The commander walked out on the deck and pointed his finger at a tiny little outboard fishing boat, where its oblivious captain was taking his time and puttering in the boat, taking up space at the dock while he organized his supplies and made sure his meager equipment was ready for the next voyage.

"One blast," the commander ordered. Jeff hit the klaxon.

It got the attention of everyone in the marina. Customers at the waterfront restaurant spilled their drinks, and dogs started barking. The poor sailor it was directed at was so startled that he nearly fell overboard. He looked over his shoulder at the idling patrol boat, quickly untied his lines, and frantically skittered out of the way.

Once moored, the commander and the crew jumped on the dock and headed to the dockmaster's office. Jeff stayed on the boat, which is his job if the boat's engines are running. He walked to the stern, where he never got tired of the sound and smell of the big diesels idling, the gurgling and burbling and the little whiffs of diesel fumes from the exhausts.

Coasties are like firefighters; they're great guys who insult each other endlessly, play pranks on each other, and talk smack and junk with anybody on the planet. The dockmaster was out, but the young woman tending the cash register had a small package waiting for the commander, so she slipped it into a paper bag and deftly handed it to him, all the while being the target of the crew's flirty and harmless trash talk and, to their great pleasure, was effortlessly and expertly dishing it right back at them.

They soon returned with drinks and snacks, unmoored the boat, and Jeff followed the commander's orders to an inlet three miles away where they dropped anchor.

The swells and breeze were light as the commander and two of the crew disappeared into the cramped quarters below deck. While they idled, Jeff manned the helm and daydreamed until the radio interrupted with an urgent message that required the commander's attention. Jeff went to the door leading to the lower deck to summon the commander, who was hunched over a tiny table with the two other crewmen.

Jeff looked carefully before he got the commander's attention. The three men had dumped the contents of the paper bag on the table and were using their service knives to divide it into tiny piles and slip it into tiny plastic bags.

Jeff was so stunned he didn't know what to do.

"Commander, sir," he said, "radio for you."

The commander, startled, whipped his head toward the open doorway, almost angrily. He quickly came up the steps and looked Jeff in the eye.

"Now you know what a 'Code White' is," he said. "What happens on this boat stays on this boat, is that clear, Coast Guardsman?"

"Yes, sir, absolutely, sir, my job is to drive this boat. None of the rest is my business."

About ten days later, they returned to the little island marina where the fuel dock was more deserted than their last visit. As usual, they entered the marina with great flourish, a "Code White" was declared, and the commander and his team jumped off as soon as they docked.

Jeff stayed behind as usual but watched through his binoculars at the easy-going behavior in the dockmaster's office, where it was manned again by the same woman as before. Lots of arm-waving and laughing.

"Thanks, Alyson," the commander said when he announced it was time to go, and the little squad swaggered out the door with a big laugh, a small package in the commander's right hand.

She noticed one of them had remained with the boat and the others had obviously forgotten to get him a drink. She wasn't supposed to leave the office, so she grabbed the dockmaster's radio to stay in touch, pulled an icy Pepsi from the cooler, and ran past the crew to take Jeff his drink.

The crew was merciless in its teasing of Alyson, and ruthless toward Jeff for stealing "their" girl.

But it was like lightning struck.

He was speechless and was barely able to mumble a thank you. She was smitten immediately and couldn't speak either. But she remembered the last name on his uniform, and she had friends all over town, including a secretary at the Coast Guard station who broke protocol and a bunch of rules to tell Alyson his name and how to reach him.

They became inseparable and were making big plans.

But so was the Guard leadership, who noticed Jeff had developed a special interest in accident investigation, and actually had a knack for it.

His transfer to Norfolk was approved, and he promised Alyson that she could join him as soon as he was settled.

He was assigned to a major incident response team on a big cutter. He really got the attention of the coastie brass when he led the investigation of the destruction of a ninety-foot fancy yacht whose engine room exploded, sinking the vessel in shallow water near the entrance to a Norfolk marina where it was convenient for the crew to be rescued. But it was Jeff's examination of the wreckage that revealed loosened bolts on all the fixtures where the propellor shafts entered the hull, and traces of an accelerant that definitely was not diesel fuel that had helped blow these compromised fixtures from the hull, allowing the sea water to flood the engine room, sinking it in minutes.

These were thrilling cases for Jeff, and he became the go-to expert in the Coast Guard's mid-Atlantic division. He saw dozens and dozens of sunken and destroyed vessels and developed a keen eye for telling the difference between an actual accident, the bungling of an incompetent skipper, and the deliberate sabotage of a vessel. He also learned the many clever ways to destroy a vessel and make it look like an accident, and he could always tell the difference.

He was especially intrigued by one case where he concluded that some sort of small bomb or explosive had been attached to the inside of the stern where the propeller shaft passed through the hull and wired to the starter of the vessel's inboard diesels. When the owner's son-in-law cranked the boat, the prop shaft blew off, sinking it and the boat moored next to it, and maiming the son-in-law, who had to be fished from the water before he drowned. Under Jeff's interrogation, the owner finally admitted that he had sabotaged his boat for the insurance and to get rid of his son-in-law.

And then, off the record, he told Jeff how he did it.

Jeff loved this stuff, and his investigations were so thorough that he never lost a case he presented to the Guard's leadership for prosecution. He had a stellar reputation and a heavy workload, often flying on a Guard helicopter to the scene of a still-burning vessel.

Alyson moved to Norfolk to be with him, and they settled into a comfortable life surrounded by other coasties. Their small apartment was near the Coast Guard station and within walking distance of a comfortable little bar where the locals met after work to insult one another.

His life with Alyson was wonderful. She adored him and was patient with the changing schedule required by his job.

But she had an edge. Jeff rarely drank, and certainly never did anything else because of the constant drug tests at work. But Alyson had a small, manageable addiction to cocaine. She always had some; he didn't know where she got it. She would use a little when they went to the bar, and she became the most engaging and fun person in the entire bar. She also might use just a little when they got home, and he enjoyed that a lot. *A lot.* But it didn't appear to him that she was using it regularly, just recreationally, and she never pressured him to try it.

He also made her promise she would never deliver little bags to anyone like she did to his commander. She promised with an eager smile, and he never had any reason to doubt that she had finished that part of her life.

One evening, Jeff got paged away from the little bar for what became one of the defining moments of his career.

He kissed Alyson good night, assured her he'd be alright but probably not home until tomorrow, and headed to the Coast Guard station where two helicopters crouched, their turbines whining, ready to go.

A small container ship was floundering in the Chesapeake Bay, listing to its port side, and several containers had broken loose and were floating away from the ship. The Coast Guard was launching a major effort to rescue the crew and make sure the ship and the loose containers were not a hazard to navigation, and Jeff was being sent with one of the rescue crews to board the ship and see what happened and how to save it.

His chopper arrived after all the crew except the captain had been evacuated. Jeff was lowered to the deck of the ship, which was now stable and not sinking at the moment but still listing dangerously, several more containers dangling over the side and threatening to join the others in the bay. The ship's running lights and deck lights still were on, providing just enough light to keep from getting injured. Jeff went to the bridge where he found the distraught captain.

"I'm from the Coast Guard," he said to the panicked captain. "Do you speak English?"

He replied, "A little, sir."

"Tell me what happened," Jeff said with authority, just as the radio crackled in his ear with the voice of the pilot of the hovering chopper, *"Ten minutes, no more."*

In broken English, the captain explained, waving his arms. "We were underway at ten knots when we heard two or three pops from near the port bow, loud enough to hear on the bridge," he said.

"Suddenly, several containers came loose from their moorings on the decks," he said, waving his arms some more." When they did, the ship became unstable and started to roll on its port side. We flooded the starboard bilge to get her balanced," he said, which is why she now squatted low in the water, but still leaning dangerously.

"Come with me," Jeff ordered, and he and the captain rushed out to the deck to check the damage. The noise and rotor draft and blinking strobe light of the chopper hovering in the darkness above added a level of madness to the wet and slippery deck of the ship. Jeff expected to find that the containers had not been settled properly into the complicated moorings that held them in place, and simply had come loose.

But that's not what he saw. Instead, he saw the remains of six of the mooring apparatuses; ragged, splintered metal, and not what you would expect to see of a mooring that had simply been pulled in the wrong direction.

These moorings had been destroyed by something.

Suddenly, the ship groaned, and leaned over a few more feet. Another container slipped into the darkness of the bay with a splash, bobbing with the others like square buoys. Jeff looked at the captain; he was in a panic and turned and sprinted toward the bridge where the escape boat was stored.

Jeff remained, though, captivated by what he was saw. Something out of the ordinary had happened here, but he couldn't tell what. He saw an unusual smudge on the corner of one of the containers still on board, perhaps a powder burn, and he took a rag, rubbed off the smudge and stuck it in his pocket. Perhaps a lab could analyze it.

"Five minutes, buster, we need some gas," came the voice on the radio.

The chopper wouldn't leave him, he hoped, but he wasn't sure. Anyway, he knew he couldn't stay much longer. The increasing list of the ship combined with the soft rolling of the bay made it almost impossible to stand. He should've already been off this ship, and he knew the impatient chopper crew thumping above him agreed. They could see as easily as he that the water was now encroaching on the deck, and the list was getting more pronounced.

He took some quick photos of the damaged moorings, and then his high-powered flashlight lit up a career-changing sight.

Wedged into the crack between an undamaged mooring and a container that was still on board was what appeared to be a stick of dynamite, or something else, he couldn't tell, and black electrical tape holding a timing device of some sort to it. For some reason, it hadn't blown, and in another five minutes, it would be underwater. He snapped quick photos and resisted the temptation to take the explosive as evidence, reckoning that his chopper friends probably wouldn't appreciate it.

His report, the subsequent inquiry, and trial unraveled a complex and wide spread conspiracy in the shipping industry that led to the arrests and convictions of several leading shipping company executives. They had arranged for their own ships to be sabotaged in various ways and for various reasons, usually because the ships were no longer profitable or needed expensive repairs or the owners needed cash from insurance settlements. The trials and lawsuits would continue for years.

And now, today, the thrill of being on that leaning deck of a sinking ship, and the noise and sea spray from the chopper in the darkness, and the satisfaction of his critical discovery, seemed a million miles from the green and white linoleum floor of this courtroom, where Jeff now hung his head.

The Coast Guard judges had no choice.

The exhaustive inquiry had extensive evidence, and Jeff was to blame, no doubt about it.

The bar had video cameras, but they only recorded Jeff and Alyson leaving with four people. There was no audio recording, but plenty of testimony that Alyson had brought some friends to meet Jeff. It wasn't revealed in court, but those friends made repeated trips to the bathroom to do lines of coke and were joined a couple of times by Alyson.

The little crowd got a lively coke buzz, and Jeff, who rarely drank, had a couple of margaritas just to keep up. Alyson was having a great time and, out of character, tried to coax Jeff to take a hit of coke off the tip of her finger.

"You've got five days off," she whispered sexily in his ear. "You won't get tested. Just try it. For me, baby."

He couldn't resist and took a half-hearted sniff from Alyson's finger. He was stunned at the rush.

After a few minutes, he began talking big about his great job as a big shot in the Coast Guard. Alyson's friends, who were a lot drunker and more stoned than he, teased him that he was exaggerating his job, and that he was probably a cook or a swab but surely not the guy who did anything important. When Jeff could stand no more of the ribbing, and with his virgin coke experience providing him strength and guidance, he invited the small group to take a ride on "his" boat, which was moored at the Coast Guard station only two easy blocks away.

The bar's cameras couldn't hear Alyson say, *"Honey, this'll be great fun, but you don't have to do this or prove anything. Let's just stay here and have another drink. But I'm in if you're in."*

The security camera at the Coast Guard station captured video of him entering the vehicle gate and walking in with five other adults, with Jeff pulling the arm of one of them as if to compel a reluctant person to go along. The key card system verified that Jeff had used his official Coast Guard badge to swipe open the gate. Video from another camera showed six people board a Coast Guard patrol boat, release it from its moorings, back it out of its dock, and depart.

There was no video of what happened next. The patrol boat's satellite tracking, which had been recorded and entered into evidence, showed that the boat left the small Coast Guard port and moved into the river, where its speed increased to nearly 20 knots. The boat turned southeast toward the area where the river merges into the ocean, and the speed increased to nearly 25 knots when it reached the open sea. The tracking showed the boat weaving back and forth while maintaining a steady speed. After ten minutes, the boat reversed its course and headed back in the direction of the river, but nearly a half mile outside of the normal shipping lane and at a speed approaching 30 knots.

Twenty-three minutes after the boat departed its berth, the satellite showed the boat's speed went to zero knots. There was no further movement.

Had there been a video, it would've shown the patrol boat moving at high speed in shallow water, its huge twin diesels producing a satisfying rumble that could be heard for miles, until it struck the huge rocks of the submerged jetty. The hull of the boat collapsed on the rocks, and the stern went straight in the air, threatening to flip the boat over on its back, its pair of screws spinning wildly in the air. Alyson, who was enjoying the thrill ride in the bow, was hurled nearly twenty yards through the air when the boat crashed, splashing headfirst into only six inches of water, underneath of which were jetty boulders the size of small cars. Jeff and the others were flung overboard but were not injured. He used the boat's radio to call his colleagues for help.

They found Alyson's body the next day, three hundred yards away, her head disfigured from the impact.

The judges declined to pursue a murder charge because of conflicting evidence. Jeff was the only one who knew how to operate the boat, but his friends testified that he actually was not at the helm during the final ten minutes of the fateful cruise. There was further evidence from his bloodwork that he had cocaine in his system that, when mixed with a small amount of tequila, may have made him pass out or be unable to drive the boat. His lawyer also made an effective case of how it made no sense for an experienced helmsman with sophisticated equipment and radar that showed hazards and shipping lanes to be so far off course. One of the other members of the party must've been operating the boat.

While they declined to convict him of the most heinous charges, they still laid the wood to him. He was convicted of manslaughter, theft and destruction of government property, improper operation of a government vehicle, felonious trespassing, and dereliction of duty. They also concluded that the lack of decent security at the Coast Guard station made it possible for this crime to occur, thus mitigating some of his responsibility. His penalty was dishonorable discharge, loss of his pension, and referral to the civilian DA for possible charges, but the DA declined because he harbored a deep dislike of the Coast Guard after a patrol crew tried to arrest him off the coast when they saw him empty raw sewage from his big weekend cruising boat into the ocean.

So, now, Jeff had nothing.

He emptied the apartment and loaded his stuff into the truck. Alyson's stuff, and whatever of his didn't fit, went in a dumpster.

He had to go.

So, he headed south, planning to drive until he could drive no more, or until he found a place to recover from the trauma of the trial. All he knew was boats, so he planned to hopscotch down the coast and check in on some marinas and small ports to see if he could find a job.

He finally ran out of energy at Southport, a tiny village on the North Carolina coast, and began to look around for work at the various marinas. He almost got a job as a deckhand on the state-owned passenger car ferry that crossed the river, but it was a state job and they checked and discovered the dishonorable discharge and sent him away.

After several weeks of getting nowhere, Jeff reluctantly signed on as the handyman at the town's Hampton Inn, fixing rickety air conditioners and scooping baby poop (or as the hotel called it, "fecal incidents") from the outdoor pool. He found a little trailer in the country. He got off work at three but had to carry a pager in case somebody threw up in the lobby or crammed a doll down a toilet.

After work, he would head down to the local marina, just to satisfy his itch to be near boats and the water, and would stop in for a drink at the Crazy Crab, a dingy, gross little bar that served the marina's drunks and served as sort of a bus station for people who were waiting to be picked up by a boat.

He drank a little more than he used to; why not? The only problem was getting paged after a couple of drinks, and he got a warning from the hotel manager to not respond to a page if he'd been drinking. If he ever did, he'd get fired.

Jeff always minded his own business, and stayed to himself, but he naturally befriended the bartender since they spent most of their afternoons together. After a couple of beers one afternoon, the bartender poked at him enough that he began to tell some of his coastie stories, and the creative ways some of the boat owners he'd investigated had blown up their boats for the insurance money or to get rid of a pesky son-in-law.

"So, you learned how they did it," the bartender asked, paying more attention to Jeff than usual, and ignoring the drunks at the bar who were grousing about the lousy service. "Have you ever tried it yourself, I mean to test how they did it? I guess, I mean could you teach somebody?"

Jeff sat in stunned silence for a minute, looking at his beer. He didn't know what to say. He'd never, ever thought about the question he'd just been asked.

"Umm, I'm not sure," Jeff replied. "I learned a lot about how they did it, but I don't know how they got the materials or how they practiced to make sure it would work." Then he continued with a laugh, "I guess there's always the chance that something could go really wrong, and we could blow someone to smithereens."

The bartender wasn't laughing.

"There's somebody I want you to meet."

They agreed to meet at noon the next Sunday, about an hour before the bar opened. Jeff arrived in the parking lot early and looked for signs of a set up. He didn't know what to look for, maybe a handful of black Crown Vics or an armored vehicle or other tips that the authorities were going to swoop in.

All he saw was the bartender unlock the back door and hold it open for another guy who looked like every guy you'd ever seen at a marina: dingy baseball cap, unshaven, tee shirt that needed to be trashed, dirty jeans, and dock shoes.

Jeff waited a minute, and then went in.

The bartender smiled, relieved that Jeff had shown up.

"This is Mike," the bartender said. "Mike has a problem. Maybe you can help."

Jeff looked at Mike and said hello. Mike's hat and tee shirt had the word "*Compelling*" on them.

"What's compelling about you?" Jeff asked.

Mike looked warily at the bartender, who nodded at him to continue.

"*Compelling* is my boat," Mike said. "It's a thirty-eight-foot Bertram fishing boat. I use it for deep sea fishing charters, river tours, sunset booze cruises. It's my business, but it's a shitty business."

Jeff looked at Mike, and then at the bartender.

"So, why are we here," Jeff asked.

"I can't make it anymore," Mike said. "I can't charge what I need to cover my costs. Diesel fuel is through the roof; it costs me a thousand bucks to fuel up. I dread the calls I get to go to the Gulf Stream because that's a big loser. Insurance is through the roof. They really stick you if you're hauling people on an older boat.

"And now it's time to overhaul the engines. I hold my breath on every trip that they'll get us back. When we're fishing, I have to idle into the wind so the diesel smoke and fumes don't kill my fishermen. An overhaul costs more than the boat is worth. And one of the bilge pumps burned up the other day, so the boat is taking on more water than the other pump can handle, so she's leaning a little bit to one side. I hope my customers don't notice."

"Why don't you sell it?" Jeff asked.

Mike looked him the eye with a sneer. "There's no market for a broken-down piece of shit. Most guys just run theirs into a cove somewhere, ground her, and walk away. I could take you to a dozen within a mile of here."

"So, what do you want from me," Jeff asked, knowing the answer.

"I want you to show me how to make her go away," Mike said. "I love her, but I need her gone in an accident, if you know what I mean. I got a little bit of insurance."

Jeff knew exactly. And he was surprised at how non-plussed he was to be knee deep in a criminal conspiracy and not be bothered by it.

So, they put a plan together. He gave Mike a list of items to buy, and Mike dropped them at the bar when he had them. Jeff took the stuff to his little trailer and began to experiment, using the process explained to him by the boat owner who wanted to finish off his son-in-law.

It took a few times and a couple of duds, but he finally got it right, creating reliable explosions that would be sure to blow the stern off the *Compelling*. The county sheriff came poking around; some neighbor must've been alarmed by the repeated explosions, but Jeff had packed away all his stuff by the time the cruiser came down the drive. Jeff told the deputy he'd heard the explosions also, and they were over yonder about a mile. The deputy said thanks and earnestly headed in that direction.

The plan was to make it look like the *Compelling's* remaining bilge pump malfunctioned during the night, sparking a buildup of fumes in the engine compartment that would destroy the boat. Bilge pumps on big boats like the *Compelling* have to run all the time because water is always leaking in around the propeller shafts or cracks in the hulls, even when docked. Jeff was convinced that a fire inspector would conclude the bilge pump was the problem, especially when he learned that the other one had already failed.

When Jeff was ready, they met again at the Crazy Crab.

"Are you ready to say goodbye to her?" Jeff asked. The bartender smiled sweetly at the question and looked somber, like he was mourner at a funeral home.

Mike hesitated, because he knew his next words were the *Compelling's* death warrant.

"Yep," he said.

"You gonna do it, or me?" Jeff asked.

Mike looked back and forth between Jeff and the bartender.

Jeff continued, "If it's me, it's four thousand to me and a thousand to him," nodding at the bartender. "If it's you, I'll show you how and a thousand to him."

He could tell Mike didn't want to make the choice. Finally, squirming on his barstool, he said, "You do it."

"Money's up front, partner," Jeff said, and Mike said he'd put it together somehow, and call when he had it.

"Holy shit."

"Oh my god."

Those words erupted spontaneously from the gaping mouths of Jeff and Mike as they walked together through the marina parking lot and got their first view of what happened to the *Compelling* the night before.

Jeff's preparations the previous day had gone flawlessly. He and Mike went to the boat late in the afternoon, when most of the other skippers and charter captains had tied up their boats and gone home or to a bar for the day. Jeff went down into the claustrophobic engine compartment and taped two of his gator bombs to the inside of the hull next to the bilge pump that still worked. He used some plastic wrap and duct tape to seal up the vents to keep the diesel fumes from escaping and punched a small hole in the fuel line to the starboard engine, starting a slow drip onto the floor of the engine room. The plan was for several hours of fuel to leak and fumes to accumulate so when the bombs ignited it would appear to an investigator that a spark from the failing pump ignited the fumes.

He set the timer for two a.m. and, as they departed, they loosened the mooring lines and removed the stern line altogether so the doomed vessel would be sure to sink instead of being bound to the dock. They had a drink at the Crazy Crab like any other day and went home.

While they slept fitfully, the side of the *Compelling's* hull blew apart, the explosion so devastating that she sank stern first in a matter of seconds, her bow pointed in the air, her superstructure ablaze, her rear end on the muddy bottom of the marina.

What Jeff and Mike didn't know, and which nobody really knew or even thought much about, was the gas and diesel pipes that supplied the electric pumps at the public fuel dock ran under the floorboard of the dock where the *Compelling* was docked. When her side blew, debris was hurled in every direction. who

A metal mooring cleat attached to her stern flew off like a bullet in the explosion, piercing the gas line under the dock, causing gas to gush into the marina's water. The gas spread quickly, and when it touched the flames of the *Compelling*, it ignited the water surrounding her and three other boats. The fire also rushed back into the broken pipe, where it flowed quickly to the end of the dock and blew the gas and diesel pumps off their pedestals and set the dock itself on fire.

The fire in the water spread quickly to two other boats, including a classic wooden-hulled cruiser which immediately started burning, flushing out from within the two occupants who were sleeping below deck. A famous plaintiff's attorney from Raleigh and his illicit beach lover escaped the cauldron completely naked and were found huddled together and shivering on shore by first responders, who thought it was odd that two men would hold each other like that, even under these stressful circumstances.

When Mike and Jeff arrived just after dawn, a half dozen fire trucks were still at the marina, their red lights flashing. The air was filled with the smell of gas and diesel and burned up wood, and smoke wafted from four boats, including the *Compelling,* which was still nose up, and the wooden cruiser and one other boat, both of which burned to the water line. A catamaran was anchored nearby, its sails completely burned but no further damage was obvious.

The dock was smudged in black soot. The broken gas line no longer spewed fuel because the main tank had emptied itself into the marina. What was left of the gas pump was floating in the marina, but there was no sign of the diesel pump. The end of the fuel dock was a charred mess, still smoldering.

Mike and Jeff looked at each other, and then looked back at the carnage.

"Good job," Mike said sarcastically.

"Wow," Jeff replied. "Man, who knew all this was gonna happen. I mean, I bet if we had tried, we couldn't have made this kind of mess."

As a boat owner, Mike was allowed by the authorities to slip under the yellow police tape to inspect what was left of his boat, and Jeff went with him. She was a sad sight, with what remained of her stern sitting in the mud on the bottom of the marina, her bow pointed skyward.

A fire captain approached them.

"We'll investigate," he said, "but it sure looks like something sparked the fumes in your engine compartment. Did you have any maintenance problems or anything not working right?"

Mike told him about the cranky bilge pump that was working overtime to compensate for the one that didn't work at all, and how he'd planned to replace them both when he had some money.

The fire captain nodded, accepting this was the likely cause of this mess, proud of the heroics required to save the rest of the entire marina, and relieved that nobody was injured or killed.

When they met later that day at the Crazy Crab, the bartender started laughing when they entered, and bought them beers to celebrate the *Compelling's* dramatic death and the good fortune of everyone in the small community that the marina still existed.

Then he looked Jeff dead in the eye.

"There's plenty of this kind of business. If you're interested. Just let me know."

With the bartender as his intermediary and his identify remaining a secret, small jobs started to come to Jeff. He wasn't sure how people from the surrounding three counties knew that the bartender was the gatekeeper, but about every month or six weeks the bartender would have a new job for him. They were usually cars and boats, the occasional shed or the little house of a wife's new boyfriend after the pissed off husband figured out where the bastard lived.

It was easy work, and the money was good. His gator bombs were simple to make, once he found a reliable supplier of Jet A fuel, and they never failed. The most challenging jobs were the modern cars whose sophisticated electronics made it difficult to make it look like an accident, so he just fire-bombed them and let the owner make his claim.

He also became something of an expert in the destruction of the new all-electric vehicles. They didn't have any gas to cause a fire, but they had massive lithium batteries. Jeff figured how to tinker with the batteries to cause a delayed short circuit that would cause a battery fire so hot and intense that there was nothing anybody could do to save the cars other than jump out and run for their lives. He charged extra for these because he knew everybody who bought these upscale cars was rich enough to afford his premium price.

The boats were usually small ones and, after the experience with the *Compelling*, he made sure the owners docked them away from other boats, and especially away from gas pipes.

He had a beer nearly every day at the Crazy Crab, and several months passed with no business. He wondered if he'd burned up everything that needed burning up.

Then, one day, he wandered in, and the bartender had a big envelope, a smile on his face, and some new business.

IV. THE TROOPER

Bud Grant and Jeff didn't know each other, but they'd met.

Bud was a state trooper assigned to the county, and he stopped Jeff a couple of years earlier for speeding during a crackdown on drunk drivers on the river road. They had a friendly chat on the side of the road, and Bud let him go with just a warning. Neither of them knew their lives would cross again, and they would never know they did.

Bud owned some rental houses. There were five of them, and he had inherited them from his father. Bud's sister got a beach house from their dad, and that was okay with Bud because he didn't care much for the beach.

The five houses were identical and were lined up next to each other on a big lot that was for one house only. There was a gravel drive that came off the county road and ran straight to the back of the lot, and the houses were lined up side-by-side facing the drive, so one house was next to the road and the fifth house was at the rear of the property.

Bud's dad built the houses decades ago and got a special exemption from the county to put five of them on one lot. The county approved his plan because there was a desperate need for affordable housing in the area. Rich people had infected the area, bought all the land and small homes and turned them into upscale neighborhoods that were second homes for people who wanted to be near the river and the ocean. The toll it took was terrible on the people who waited tables, fought fires, and drove the garbage trucks, and they had to move farther and farther from where they worked to serve the people who had displaced them from their affordable homes and lives.

Bud had no interest in being a landlord, but he enjoyed the steady rental income which allowed him to have a great fishing boat and some other things he couldn't afford on a trooper's salary, like a twice-yearly visit to Vegas to indulge his obsession with prostitutes, of which there were plenty at home, but a state trooper didn't last long playing that game in his own backyard.

To say he was an absentee property owner was an understatement. The rental agent who managed the property rarely talked to Bud except to ask for permission to make a repair, replace an appliance, or fix a roof. Bud usually said no, so the agent quit calling. About the only thing Bud would pay was the property taxes, and he always waited until the last minute to pay those. One year he forgot, and the houses almost got sold on the courthouse steps.

Over time, the five houses fell into disrepair, and the amount of rent that could be charged dropped as well. As the rents fell, a new category of tenant began to move in, with their cars up on blocks, garbage in the yards, and frequent visits from the cops to break up fights between husbands and wives or to bring home their teenagers who had stolen something, hit somebody, or lost their minds on meth. The place became a mess, and the complaints from neighbors to county government started to roll in.

After a couple of years of neglect by Bud and abuse by his tenants, the five houses were filthy and hardly anything in them worked.

And that's when Bud and his rental agent were summoned to a meeting with the chairman of the county commission. He, of course, knew and respected Bud as a state trooper, but something had to be done about the calamity on Bud's property.

"Bud, I'm sorry, but this is complicated," the county manager said. "You have no idea how complicated."

Bud sat and listened, his uniform pressed and his smokey bear hat in his hand. He always wore his uniform to meetings of any kind, because it intimidated nearly everyone.

The county manager explained that when the special exemption for the property was granted to Bud's father to build five houses on one lot, several stipulations were included. The most important one, the chairman explained, required the property to be maintained at certain standards. These standards were spelled out, and they clearly were not being met.

The chairman paused and looked Bud in the eye.

"Here's the deal, Bud," the chairman said. "You haven't met the terms of the special exemption, not even close, and not for years. They don't even meet county code anymore, must less the special exemption. Those houses are junk and the people living in them are junk, and they are living in conditions that are an embarrassment to the county. Bud, I drove down the driveway the other day, and the smell alone was awful. Either you fix them and get them back to standard, or the county condemns them and takes them from you. And you'll have nothing. I'm serious about this, Bud."

Bud sat stunned and looked at his agent. He never thought about losing the houses and the income they produced, even the meager amount he had received lately.

He was still digesting this news and these prospects when the chairman continued.

"Bud, you need to think about your place in this community," he said. "You've given most everybody a ticket for something at one time or another, but you really are respected. You've pulled their drunk kids out of wrecked cars and had to go to some of their houses with the worst news they ever received. You're an icon in this town, and you need to think about that, because I think nobody's gonna respect you if you continue to ignore these shitholes you own. Figure out what you want to do and let me know. Before the end of the week."

Bud and his agent left the building and stood on the sidewalk. He looked at the agent, and his eyes said, *"What do I do?"*

The agent opened his padfolio.

"Bud, I've done some preliminary math," he said. "It's gonna cost at least twenty-five thousand."

Bud smiled, "That's not so bad."

"Per house," the agent said. "That's a buck twenty-five, at least. Plus, we'll have to evict everyone while you fix them up, so you lose the rental income during that period of time. And it could cost more, Bud, this is just a guess. Who knows what we'll find when we start the work."

Bud dropped his head, his chin resting on the chest of his splendid uniform.

"It's not all bad, Bud," the agent said, as if he was comforting a new widower at the funeral home. "Thanks to me, you have great insurance coverage. I've never told you all the gory details, but I made sure you were insured, and those premiums were paid. They're covered at two hundred thousand a piece if anything happens to them."

Bud didn't need the agent to help him with that math.

They had to go.

"So, whatta we do?" Bud asked, his brain spinning.

"How about I take care of it," his agent replied. "No questions asked. A state trooper doesn't need to be involved in this shit."

Bud looked at him like the agent was speaking in tongues.

"I'm taking a huge chance right here on this sidewalk," the agent said. "I'm talking to a law enforcement officer about something pretty damned illegal. You might could arrest me right here, but I don't think you will because you've got nowhere to go. And remember, no questions asked. You don't want to know, and you can't arrest me if you don't know anything."

Bud's shoulders slumped. He looked at the agent and nodded slightly.

"I can make 'em go away," the agent said. "But it costs a lot of money."

"Like how much?" Bud asked. The agent said twenty-five thousand, cash.

Bud winced. *I don't have it, and can't get it,* he said.

"So how about this," the agent said, lowering his voice. "I'll cover the up front, and you split the insurance with me. Whatever you get from insurance, we split 50-50. It's a risk for both of us, because you never know with insurance companies. But this is the best offer you're gonna get."

Bud looked at the ground, in denial about what was happening. He looked up and nodded again.

"Put this out of your mind," the agent said. "The next thing you hear will be a call that something bad has happened to your rental houses."

"Do we need to shake on it?" he asked his agent.

"Naw," the agent replied, grinning. "We're men of honor."

Jeff made his daily stop at the Crab Shack. The bartender was grinning. Some business had walked through the door, the bartender said. It looks legit. The package is thick, feels like money inside.

He always walked in through the back door after sitting in his truck and watching the Crab Shack for a few minutes to ensure no strangers were lurking about and sat at the far end of the bar. It was three o'clock, and the place was mostly empty except for two hard-core drunks drinking straight vodka and a couple who hoped the darkness of the bar would disguise their illicit rendezvous.

The bartender set a draft beer and a manila envelope in front of Jeff. The only thing he said to Jeff was, "I told the guy he needed to make sure the electricity stayed on. Same message I give everybody."

Jeff nodded, took a sip of the beer, then opened the big envelope. He peered into it, and without removing the cash, he thumbed through it and saw it should be about right. He counted out a thousand and slid it across the bar to the bartender, took another sip of beer, and left out the back door.

When he got to his trailer, he dumped out the contents of the envelope, including the cash and a written description of the job.

He was flabbergasted. Aghast. Confused about what to do. And thoroughly challenged and thrilled by what he saw.

Five houses, all next to one another. To be accidentally destroyed by fire. All of them.

The houses would be empty. The occupants had been evicted. It's probably unusual for an arsonist to have a moral compass, but his rule was that he never torched a building or a boat that occupied by a person or an animal, at least that he knew of. Nobody or nothing was gonna get hurt by him just so somebody could get rid of their stuff and collect an insurance check. So, whoever the client was knew this since they made a point of mentioning it. Perhaps a repeat customer, Jeff thought.

His next move was to do a drive by and see what the target looked like. He had the address and drove by a couple of times before turning into the gravel driveway. The houses were in horrible condition, and the yards were filled with junk and furniture that the evicted occupants left behind.

Jeff had never been confronted with such an audacious job. Five houses, all unoccupied, needed to catch fire at once. Get completely destroyed. And look like an accident.

So, Jeff responded to an audacious job with an audacious plan that would get a boost from nature, and that help was brewing two hundred miles off the coast. A category 1 hurricane was swirling out there and might become a Cat 2 before it hit the coast just a few miles south of Bud's property.

Jeff's plan was to salt each house with a few of his specialty gator bombs. The timers ignited a regular old M80 firecracker inside the Gatorade bottle that lit up the jet fuel and all hell broke loose. His backyard tests had been flawless.

And he was going to get lucky with the storm, because downed power lines and falling trees can cause all sorts of havoc, including unfortunate house fires, and firefighters would be so busy they couldn't respond quickly. If he timed it correctly, they might not respond at all if the storm was bad enough because not even first responders venture out in the height of a storm.

Also, if his calculations were accurate, the direction of the prevailing winds from the approaching storm would make it appear that they pushed the blaze from one house to another.

To make sure things went according to plan, Jeff went to the property late one afternoon and quickly used a chain saw to cut a notch in a skinny pine tree next to the first house, hoping that the storm's winds would send the weakened tree onto the roof and powerline of the first house.

It would be a perfect storm. Jeff grinned at the irony.

As the weather worsened, Jeff watched the television coverage constantly, because timing was going to be everything on this job. Hurricane Barry was forecast to hit the shoreline as a weak Cat 2 storm, with winds topping out in the ninety mile per hour range, which was perfect for Jeff but unlucky for anyone who owned a home on the beach or riverfront. Barry had zigged a little bit in the last twelve hours, so it was going to hit the coast slightly north of original expectations, but that would have no effect on Jeff's work.

Landfall would be around two the next morning, so Jeff gathered his supplies and loaded them in a pair of Igloo coolers as the winds picked up and darkness began to fall. His plan was to be at Bud's dilapidated houses as the storm peaked.

The forecasters remained confident in the timing of landfall, so Jeff headed toward Bud's property around one.

As he carefully drove towards his targets, he mused about how there's nothing like being in a hurricane. The wind blew the rain, leaves and pine straw sideways. There was always the danger of a tree suddenly being blown over onto the road and smashing him and his truck flat. He'd heard of that happening to firefighters and others in the past, and it's why he was mostly alone right now. Off in the distance, there were brief pops of bright light as electric transformers blew up. One of the most unique things about a hurricane, he thought, was the smell, the tropical scent of the rain, and the unmistakable rich aroma of freshly broken and destroyed pine trees. He thought, *There's nothing like it. It's terrifying but spectacular.*

He parked in the woods across the road from Bud's junk

and pulled his coolers from the truck. He had a moment of dread as he looked and saw the tall pines bending violently in the wind, and hoped he was somewhere else when they snapped.

Crossing the road, he was pleased to see that his notched pine had already crashed onto the roof of the first house and was leaning on the power line. Perfect.

He kicked in the door and got a brief reprieve from the wind and rain. The inside of the house was dark and smelled like mold and piss. He knew his plan, but he took a minute to review it in his mind. He had twenty of his little gator bombs, each filled with Jet A and topped with an M80 and a timer. Four bombs per house, one in each corner of the main living area. He figured it would take him about eight minutes per house, so he set the timers in the first house for forty-five minutes, and then eight minutes less in each house so that the houses would explode at about the same time. If he calculated correctly, he would have time to set his bombs and leave the area before they exploded.

So, he went to work. He placed his little bombs in the corners of the main room of the first house, set the timers as a heavy squall beat on the side of the smelly house, then slipped back into the wind and rain. He was soaked, but the Igloos kept his arsenal dry. He repeated the process at the second, third and fourth houses, careful to adjust the timers properly at each spot.

He finished his work on the fourth house, and stepped onto the porch, ready for another dash through the storm to his final victim. But something caught his eye as he looked toward the fifth house. A light was coming from inside, and it was flickering. His mind was racing. Had something, the storm perhaps, already set this house on fire?

He moved through the wind and rain toward the fifth house, pulling one of the coolers with him. He stepped up to the front window, and looked in.

There was a small fire in the middle of the room, almost like a campfire, with its smoke drifting toward an open window at the rear of the house.

A woman sat cross-legged on the floor, rocking back and forth, staring at the little blaze. Her hair looked unkempt, and she was barefooted.

The clock in Jeff's head screamed at him that he had only a couple of minutes to figure this out.

He slowly opened the door, and the woman whipped her head toward him, her face a terrified mess, her mouth opened but no scream came out. She skittled on her hands and knees like a crab toward the opposite end of the room, into the corner, cowering in fear, trying to get away from Jeff.

He held up his hands. *I'm not going to hurt you.*

"What are you doing here?" he yelled at her over the furious sounds of the storm. "You've got to get out! Now!"

The clock in his head was ticking. All hell was going to break loose in about two minutes, but he'd actually lost count.

He moved toward her, not exactly sure what he'd do when he got to her. He couldn't hurt her, but he sure couldn't leave her here and he wasn't excited at all that she'd seen his face.

"This is not safe," he screamed at her. "Please go!"

She refused to move. So, Jeff went around the room, placed his little bombs, and added an extra minute to the timer so he could deal with her, but he was distracted as he set the final gator bomb.

He moved toward her and grabbed her skinny arm. "You're coming with me."

He wrenched her from the corner, pulled her to the front porch and then out onto the gravel drive, the wind hitting him in the face like tiny needles, and the sounds of the storm intensifying and becoming more terrifying, with the loud, horrifying snap of trees breaking all around them, the thump of huge limbs hitting the ground.

He couldn't see her very well; he thought again, there is nothing darker than a nighttime hurricane.

She was so skinny that she was easy to pull up the gravel drive. She didn't really resist, but she wasn't cooperating either, just kind of dragging along.

Then they started to pop.

The timers on the little bombs weren't perfectly synchronized, so it sounded like a barrage of heavy gunfire as they ignited, and then they went totally silent. Jeff and the woman were nearly to the main road, and they both turned toward the houses, he to admire his work, she to be further shocked.

The bombs had done their jobs. The houses were ablaze, the intense flames overcoming the heavy rain's attempt to extinguish them, the wind so strong that the nearby woods would've been threatened by the fire had they not been drenched by the storm.

He could finally see her in the light of the fires, and could see she was bedraggled, probably homeless, terrified, and awfully skinny.

"Go!" he shouted to her and pointed down the road. "Go! Find someplace else! I can't help you!"

She half crawled, half stumbled down the drenched and dark road, covered in leaves and tree branches, the rain and wind punishing her tiny frame.

It broke his heart. *I can't just walk away.*

He was conflicted, torn about what to do. He reached for his door handle but turned and looked back at her as she half crawled, half stumbled down the road, the rain and wind punishing her tiny frame.

His thoughts ripped through his brain. *If I leave her, she might die in this storm, and I'm not sure my soul can take another death. Maybe I can drop her at the hospital, just dump her on the curb, or maybe the courthouse. Somebody will find her. But she's seen my face, and seen my truck, and may not care that I saved her life. Maybe there'd be a reason why she'd keep quiet, but maybe not. Can I take that risk?*

Then, staccato lightning, adding another level of terror to the night.

Again, like strobe lights, lightning flashes in rapid succession, with ominous and horrifying possibilities.

He'd heard about it in the Coast Guard. When a tornado forms inside a massive thunderstorm or a hurricane, it produces staccato lightning unlike anything in a routine summer rainstorm. The intense, frenetic pulses of lightning are a warning that something terrible is nearby.

As he desperately thought about the options for the pitiful wretch in the road, it happened again, the pulses so manic and intense that he thought he would have a stroke. And, then he heard it, even louder than the chaos of the hurricane, the sound they all talk about, the train roaring through the night.

He ran toward the woman, and grabbed her frail arm, dragging her back to the truck, opening the passenger door and dumping her on the floorboard of the passenger seat. He fell on top of her just as the truck started rocking violently, as if seized by some mammoth hand that was shaking it to pieces. The sound was unbelievable; the tornado's winds flung pinecones and tree branches at the truck, the sound of bullets hitting their target. He had no idea what was hitting the truck, or how long the truck would survive this onslaught. For a moment, if felt like the truck was moving, like the mammoth hand was shifting it, sliding it from its parking space.

And then it was over.

The only sound was that of the hurricane, and the lightning had moved on to terrorize someone else.

He cautiously lifted his head, and then sat straight up, not believing what he saw.

The first two houses were gone, no fire, no nothing. Just gone. The third house had no roof and had mostly collapsed and its fire was smoldering. It looked like a bunch of debris has smashed into the side of the fourth house, which still burned, and the fifth house was missing its roof and most of the first floor but was completely ablaze, providing the light needed for him to get a dim view of what happened.

It took a moment for his mind to comprehend what he saw, and he briefly thought about how ironic this scene was because the hurricane and tornado mostly took care of his job tonight. But he also realized that if those houses had been occupied, the families who had lived in them would be dead right now, their bodies to be found later miles away scattered in trees and ditches by a tornado that dropped down on them.

I need to get out of here, he finally concluded. Help might be on the way, and I need to be somewhere else.

He took the woman to the Hampton Inn. It had no power, naturally, but all the guests and employees had been subject to a mandatory evacuation, so the place was deserted. He used his pass key to enter the lobby and grabbed two flashlights from his workroom before using another special key to unlock a room since the key card reading system was disabled.

She still hadn't spoken and looked around the room as if she was entering a prison.

"You'll be safe here," he said. "The water still runs, but probably no hot water. Why don't you sleep, and I'll check on you tomorrow."

She still said nothing, but looked at the bed, and lay down, closed her eyes, and slept immediately. He left.

He checked on her for the next two days, and she still said nothing, but looked better. Obviously, sleep was helping. He brought her some food; the Waffle House down the road never stopped doing its smothered and covered thing even at the height of the storm, so he brought her eggs and toast and when he returned her takeout box was always empty. When the hotel staff returned, he made arrangements for her to stay, and they were always helpful when someone was a refugee and needed a room. Besides, no vacationers were coming to this town for a long time.

On the fifth day, he came to see her, and figured it was time for something to happen. She couldn't stay at the Hampton forever, and he wasn't sure what to do.

He entered the room, and she had opened the curtain to the window that overlooked the hotel's small swimming pool, and was standing there, gazing out. It looked like she had bathed, and her hair was wet. Good signs, he thought.

"Hello," he said. "How are you feeling?"

She turned, not startled by this arrival.

"Mira," she said.

"Mirror?"

"No," she replied patiently, "Mira."

He still didn't understand.

"Mira," she said more emphatically. "That's my name. I'm Mirabelle, but everyone calls me Mira."

Well, this is progress, Jeff thought.

"I'm Jeff," he said.

She smiled. "I needed that storm, and I needed someone to save me."

"What do you mean?"

"I was in that house to kill myself," she said. "I was so badly messed up on meth that I couldn't see a way out. No money for more meth, no place to live. I knew those places were empty. I had the fire going and was going to OD on some sleeping pills and let the place burn down around me.

"You dragged me out before I took the pills. I was waiting to make sure I didn't fuck up the fire. And then I was so relieved when you let me go, and sent me down the road, so I could finish what I started. I had the pills in my hand when you grabbed me. That storm probably would've killed me."

She told him that her brain was fried that night; she tried to speak, but nothing would come out. The last five days had been hell as her body started to recover from the meth, and she realized that she couldn't get any because of the storm.

She felt better now, and he was the reason.

"I need to go home," she finally said, "back to Florida."

She told him a long story of a broken home, and being raised by a colorful, overbearing aunt who tried to control her and finally drove her away. She was vague about how she ended up in this small coastal town, hooked on meth, and trying to end it all in the middle of a hurricane.

"I'll help you," Jeff said, not remotely certain about how he could. "You can stay at my trailer while you rest up. I'm not a creep, and you'll be safe."

"And we'll think of some way to get you home."

Bud was supposed to be on a fishing trip this week, but all leaves were cancelled because of the storm, so he was on duty and would be all night and way into tomorrow.

There really wasn't much he could do, and there wasn't any traffic on the roads because of a mandatory curfew. Everybody heeded the experts' pleas to stay home. He parked his cruiser under the overhang of a bank drive-through to keep any trees from crashing on him, and to get a break from the relentless onslaught of the wind and rain. His personal phone buzzed. It was the local fire chief.

"Bud, man, I hate this," the chief said, "but your rentals are on fire. We just got the call. Said it looked like a tree hit the powerline, and the wind spread the fire. I'm sorry, man, but we can't do anything until the sustained winds drop below 70."

Bud thanked him for the call, and said he understood the rules during a storm were for everyone's safety, and that's just how it was.

When he hung up, he decided to go see for himself. He flipped on his blue lights and headed toward his houses, having to go slowly around downed trees. He passed one truck that was headed toward town. Under different circumstances, he'd pull him over and see why the driver was out in the middle of a hurricane.

As he approached the houses, the rain was falling so heavily that it reflected the blue lights and nearly blinded him, so he switched them off. Tree limbs cluttered the road, and lots of debris. He hit something so hard that it twisted the steering wheel in his hand, perhaps a tree limb, or maybe a deer or something that was fleeing the storm.

He pulled into the gravel drive of his property. Two of the houses were completely gone, just blackened cinder block foundations, some smoke still drifting into the winds of the storm. The other three were destroyed, with some flames still eating away at them, acrid smoke mixing with the damp, pine scent of the hurricane.

He backed out and returned to the bank drive-through to wait for dawn. He thought about the beauty of days after a storm, when the skies are bright blue, and the humidity has been swept away by the fury of the storm. It was always a relief after the gruesome horror of a nighttime storm.

It took about sixty days for the insurance company to process his claim. He got a call from his rental agent, and they arranged to meet.

"Whatta mean my share is only a hundred grand?" Bud asked, really angry.

The agent was surprised by Bud's reaction. He thought Bud would be happy with anything.

"Well," the agent said, "the company agreed to two hundred and you and I agreed to split it. End of story."

"I thought they were insured for a million," Bud said, really getting angry. "That's what you told me! A hundred ain't five hundred!"

The agent reminded Bud that he had fronted the twenty-five to get the job done, so he wasn't getting a full share anyway.

Then he slowly walked Bud through the process, like he was talking to a third grader, using lots of insurance jargon that made no sense to Bud.

What he didn't tell Bud was that the insurance company had approved the million-dollar claim, but the agent and his regional supervisor doctored the documents to show a two-hundred thousand settlement and split the rest of the eight hundred between them. The agent also never told his supervisor that he was splitting Bud's share also.

"This was hardly worth it," Bud said, and stormed out, frustrated but happy that he was no longer a slumlord.

A few days later, Bud was at an incident on the main beach road where an all-electric Tesla had suddenly incinerated itself in the middle of the road. The local fire department had no idea how to extinguish a fire involving a car that was mostly a big lithium battery, so they let it burn until it was a smoldering and crackling pile of aluminum and wires. Bud was trying to untangle the traffic backup, mostly from folks who slowed to a crawl to watch a car burn up.

When a wrecker finally dragged the melted pile of former Tesla parts out of the road, the fire chief came over to Bud.

"I got news for you, buddy," the chief said.

"Yeah, what," Bud replied, barely listening, as he removed his reflective safety vest.

"You got firebombed."

Bud stopped what he was doing and looked at the chief.

"What?"

"Yep, your rentals got bombed, and I got the evidence," the chief said.

Bud felt sick at his stomach. He knew what happened to his rentals, but how did the chief know? And how much more did the chief know?

"We found one of the little bombs," the chief said with a big grin. "It was in the rubble of the house farthest from the road. Looks like it didn't blow up. We found it when we were combing for clues."

Bud was dumbfounded and confused. How could this happen, especially since those houses burned so thoroughly. And if the chief could prove it was arson, would he have to give back the insurance money? He had no idea what any of this meant.

"It's an old plastic drink bottle, filled with high-octane gas of some sort," the chief continued. "Had a little timer on it. It scared us so bad we called in the state bomb squad, and they looked at it and thought it was best to just blow it up in that fancy rig they have. And guess what they found before the blew it up?

"I don't know," Bud replied, afraid of the answer.

"A fingerprint."

Even though Bud had been on the overnight shift and had been busy with wrecks and a drunk fight at a bar, he couldn't sleep when he got home.

He was always exhausted after these overnight gigs, but every time he drifted off to sleep, he awoke with a start and sat up in his bed, thinking back on his conversation with the fire chief and the horrifying implications of a single fingerprint.

He thought about what would happen if they caught the guy, and he knew they could find anybody with even a partial fingerprint. He wondered if they'd gotten any DNA off the bomb before they blew it up, and he sure hoped not, because DNA sends more guys to prison than anything else.

What if they caught him, and what if he talked? What if he coughed up the name of the rental agent who hired him, and that guy was so sleezy that he'd hand over Bud in a minute? That story would be news across the region: State trooper implicated in arson scheme. And then there was the insurance fraud. Good lord, Bud thought, and got up to toss down a double dose of Alka Seltzer.

He couldn't sleep, so he put on a fresh uniform and sent a message to the command center that he was returning to duty.

Basically, he was just riding around to take his mind off things. Not much was happening on the roads today, and then he saw the flashy Suburban of his rental agent, with his name and photo on the rear windows and his cell number in big white letters.

He did a U-turn, and flipped on his blue lights.

"What the fuck, Bud," the agent said when the trooper approached the driver's window.

"We need to talk," Bud said.

"Why can't you call like a normal person?

"I want to talk now, in privacy. Get in."

The agent grunted impatiently, and squeezed into the cluttered passenger seat of Bud's patrol car, which he shared with a laptop computer and various other things Bud needed to do his job.

"This is bad advertising, to have me pulled over like this," the agent said.

"Shut up, we've got an issue."

When Bud told him that one of bombs was confiscated and they found a finger print, the agent tried to roll down his window, but it was locked, so Bud had to do it and just in time as the agent wretched out the window.

"Oh my god," the agent said.

"No shit," replied Bud. "How vulnerable are we? If they catch this guy you hired, what's he gonna do? What does he know?"

The agent thought for a moment and wiped the stinky spittle from the corner of his mouth with the sleeve of his monogrammed shirt.

"You know, I think we're okay," he said, but not very reassuringly. "Obviously the deal was done in cash, and he never knew my name and I never knew his. We never met. We dropped the cash and info at the Crazy Crab, and I had one of my ignorant associates do that, but that would be easy for the cops to piece together. I guess the bartender saw who made the drop, but bartenders are notorious for their short memories."

Bud felt a little better, but not a lot. A ding on his computer broke the silence: overturned vehicle in a roadside ditch, unknown number of victims trapped inside. Fire and rescue enroute. Code 1.

"I gotta go," Bud said. "You're free to go," he added with a sneer, and unlocked the passenger door.

Jeff's house guest was improving. He felt comfortable leaving her while he went to work and wasn't worried about her stealing stuff because he didn't really have anything to steal. His cash was well-hidden, so no worries there.

If she disappeared one day while he was away, it would actually be okay. He knew this arrangement couldn't and shouldn't last, but he felt good that he was helping someone after all the horrible things he'd done.

He also resumed his regular stops at the Crazy Crab, but his side hustle had dried up and he was okay with that also. Things needed to settle down a little; there were still hard feelings about the marina fire and lots of pressure on the fire chief to figure out a cause. Nobody believed the deal that a self-destructing bilge pump could unleash that kind of mayhem.

"I heard some stuff you need to know," the bartender said one afternoon as he eased into his usual spot."

"Okay, let's hear it."

"First, the rumor among the firemen who come in here is they found a bomb in what was left of one of Bud's houses," the bartender said as Jeff almost choked on his light beer.

"And, that's not all," he continued. "They found a fingerprint on it, and then a bomb squad blew it up."

The bartender stared at Jeff, waiting for some kind of reaction.

"I wonder if they can find somebody with one fingerprint," Jeff asked, not expecting the bartender to have any idea.

"I bet so," was the reply.

Jeff was trying to not panic, but he looked at his beer can. Hell, his fingerprints were all over it. And all over dozens of beer cans in the recycling dumpster out back.

He thought hard about whether he'd ever been fingerprinted. His shoulders sagged as he remembered having his prints taken during his induction into the Coast Guard. He wondered if the Guard shared that kind of stuff with civilian authorities.

"Whatcha thinking," the bartender asked, casually wiping the bar with a dingy rag.

"I'm glad you've got good ears," he said, smiling at the bartender. "You hear a lot of useful stuff."

"That's what I get paid for," he replied. "But I'm not very good at giving advice on what to do with it."

Jeff smiled back.

He had already decided what to do.

It was the first time he and Mira had talked about the night of the fires, other than what she was planning to do. She never asked what he was doing there, or if he was the cause of the fires. She wasn't stupid, he could tell, but it was clear that night was a mess in her brain and her memory.

"You know, I did some things that night that might get me in trouble," he told her. "I've done other things also."

She listened but didn't speak.

"I might need to leave," he told her. "In fact, I'm pretty sure I need to. I'm not sure, but I might be in trouble. You might end up on your own again. What will you do?"

She looked back at him, with a look that came as close to warmth as anything he'd seen from her.

"I know what I'll do," she said. "Perhaps it's what *we* should do."

"What's that mean?"

V. THE MANAGER

She was in the bunk of her catamaran sailboat docked at the marina where she often retreated to drink good scotch and escape from the complaints about high taxes, yard debris, and non-responsive government, and those were just the complaints of her drunk and worthless husband.

Pauline was the county manager, a rarity for a woman in this part of the world, and every now and then she needed to get away, and her catamaran was just the place.

She was an excellent sailor, a skill she learned in prep school, but she rarely took her boat anywhere because that would be too much work and distract her from the real purposes of these escapes, which were to drink a bottle of scotch, escape from the angry, seething bastard she lived with, and get a break from everything.

She usually had company on her boat, and they were usually young. Tonight's guest was a handsome teenaged bag boy from the Harris Teeter, with whom she'd been flirting for several weeks before demurely asking him if he'd ever slept on a boat. He got the message instantly, and his parents were satisfied that he was at a friend's house.

She had just dozed off, finally relaxed with a belly brimming with Macallan 18, the gentle rocking of the boat soothing her troubled soul, and the smooth arms of the teenager around her naked waist, when a powerful clap startled her awake, and a bright flickering light burst through the port hole. Her brain was too scrambled from the scotch and frenzied albeit brief lovemaking to immediately know what was happening, but her jumbled thoughts were that a thunderstorm was rolling through and that's what woke her up.

The acrid smell of smoke, though, sobered her instantly, and she immediately assumed that her beloved catamaran was on fire. She grabbed some shorts and a tee shirt and scurried up the narrow steps to the deck of the boat, followed by the teenager who was awkwardly wriggling into his shorts, and to a scene that neither of them could process.

It looked like the entire marina was on fire, and the boat moored next to hers was quickly sinking.

What mattered the most was that her sails were on fire.

She rushed back below deck and groped around in the darkness for her tiny marine fire extinguisher. She found it, finally, and returned to her sails, which were melting more than burning. What was left of them was dripping onto the decks, and she wondered what in the world they were made of to make them melt like that.

She looked around at the chaos. Gas was pouring out from

under the dock, spewing like a flamethrower, and the water was on fire. In addition to the boat next to hers, two other boats were burning, and it looked like two naked men were fleeing one of them, holding hands.

Pauline quickly decided she needed to save her boat, and looked around for the bag boy to help her, but he was sprinting up the footpath toward the parking lot. She cursed him under her breath, and jumped onto the dock where she released the mooring lines at the bow and stern. She put one foot on her boat and another on the dock and pushed as hard as she could before scrambling back onto the boat. It slowly drifted from the dock until she got the small engine started, and then started backing it out, parallel to the dock, and past the other boats tied up.

She thought she was in the clear as she crept by the end of the dock where the fuel pumps were, but they exploded, shocking her senseless, blinding her from the flash, and spraying her with gas and little chunks of debris. There was a huge thump, when the smoking carcass of the top half of the diesel pump fell out of the air, splashing into the water, spraying her with diesel fuel and filthy water.

She was so stunned she just stood and screamed as her catamaran continued to putter stern first out of the burning marina.

Typically, a fire department does an assessment of a major incident, including the likely cause, how it could've been prevented, how the department responded, and how its equipment and personnel performed. These reports usually included some lessons learned, and almost always identified the need for some new piece of expensive equipment that would've saved the day had the department already owned it.

Pauline read the initial report from the marina disaster, and she was completely dissatisfied.

And that's why today's group was in her office.

She had summoned the chiefs of the five fire departments that cover the county. They all responded to the marina fire. Also at her conference table was the county attorney and, sitting at the end opposite from Pauline, was Amos Andrews, the richest guy in the area. He owned the marina and most of the vacation rentals in the county, and he flew in from his winter home in Florida to personally inspect what was left of his marina and to attend this meeting with Pauline.

She looked at the town's fire chief and nodded. The chief cleared his throat and opened his file.

"Our investigation showed that a cruiser named the *Compelling* was tied up at the dock and suffered a mechanical problem or electrical short that ignited a buildup of diesel fumes in the engine compartment," the chief read from his report. "The boat exploded, and debris cut the gas pipe, discharging gas into the water of the marina where it ignited and subsequently spread to three other boats, including yours, Missus Commissioner, and to the fuel pumps, which were destroyed. The first truck was on scene three minutes after we got the call, and a mutual aid call was immediately sent. No one was killed or injured, even though we did administer aid and comfort to two gentlemen from one of the boats, and no fire department equipment was damaged or destroyed during the incident."

Pauline looked over the top of her reading glasses, "Anything else, chief?"

"No ma'am, that about sums it up," the chief replied, thumbing through his file looking for anything else but knowing there was nothing.

Pauline looked at the county attorney. "Tell them what you told me."

The attorney pulled out his notes and spoke precisely and somberly.

"There is no coastal community our size in the entire United States of America that has as many marine damage insurance claims as our little community right here," he said. He paused for a moment to let that sink in, so to speak.

He continued.

"Let me re-phrase to make it clear. The boat owners in our county file nearly twice the number of insurance claims than anywhere else our size in the entire country. It's interesting that the number of claims for stupid stuff is about average, stuff like overturned boats, boats that hit rocks, boats that hit each other, those claims are about average.

"But what's *not* average is the boats that are destroyed by fire or explosion. We are an outlier in the entire country. Over the last five years, our average number of these claims is twice the average for a place our size. Something's going on, but I don't know what."

He paused and look around the room. The fire chiefs said nothing.

Amos slammed his hand on the table.

"This is goddamn intolerable!" he shouted. "If this keeps up, nobody'll be able to afford insurance if they can get it at all! My insurance company said it'll pay my claim on the marina, but if I file the claim, they made it clear they'll cancel my policy going forward. They see the same numbers and trends and all they see is this county is a damned fire hazard."

When Amos spoke, people listened. When he yelled, they cowered. He was the richest and most powerful guy in the county, but also the most generous. His charitable gifts were legendary, and the fire chiefs at the table knew very well that each of their departments had trucks that he quietly paid for and firefighters who went to sophisticated training programs because he wrote the checks.

"Listen, people," Amos said, leaning forward. "Why would anybody sailing their shitty little boat from New York to Florida for the winter spend the night at our little marina, buy our gas, eat in our restaurants, buy crap at the little shops, if they're worried they're gonna be fried to a crisp while they're sleeping in their boat? Forget the insurance problem. We can't have that kind of reputation!"

Everyone nodded soberly. The local chief spoke up.

"We do see a lot of boat fires, and there may be some we don't even know about that are put out by the owners, or the boat sinks and there's nothing to put out, so they don't call us," he said. "But when we do get a call, these boat fires are impossible to investigate. If an engine room blows, there's nothing left. And every skipper who has an inboard engine knows he's gotta blow the fan before cranking it to keep it from blowing. It's hard to believe there's that many idiots out there."

Amos slammed his hand again.

"So, Pauline, what're we gonna do about this?" he yelled again.

Pauline squirmed in her chair, knowing that Amos put her in this chair and could take her out of it.

"Here's an idea," Pauline said, "if for no other reason than to reassure the insurance companies. We'll appoint a committee, a high-profile one, do a big story in the paper and everything. They'll be charged with reviewing every boat incident in the last couple of years and look for any trends and see if there's any fraud or anything. See if they can learn about the finances of the boat owners, see what was going on."

Amos slumped in his chair, deflated.

"Is that all you got?" he asked, glaring at Pauline.

"That's all I got," she said. "I'm open to ideas."

Amos raised up out of this seat and headed for the door.

"I'm going back to South Carolina," he said. "You've got three months to figure this out."

And he walked out and slammed the door.

Amos headed to the county's airport where his Citation was fueled and waiting for him, and to a meeting he'd already set up. It would be in a dumpy meeting room in the building they called a terminal, and it would only last five minutes.

He walked into the building, where his pilots were standing, arms crossed, ready to go. He could hear the high-pitched whine of his plane's auxiliary power unit, keeping the luxurious interior comfortable until its owner decided he was ready.

"Five minutes," he said to the pilots, and one of them turned and headed to the plane without speaking.

Amos opened the door to the meeting room where his guest was waiting.

"Well," Amos said, "it went about like expected. They've got no idea what's going on or what to do about it."

"So," he continued, "it's your turn."

The private investigator looked back at him with that look that all private investigators have, a kind of supreme confidence mixed with bored nonchalance as if they've seen everything and done most everything.

"The issue isn't really complicated," he said. "People are burning their own boats for money. But why so many here is more complicated. So, what's your expectation? What do you want for your money?" the PI asked.

"Find out if these damned boat owners have learned from each other how to scam the insurance companies," Amos said. "Hell, there might be a damned school that they're all going to, I don't know. See if somebody's teaching them and tell me who he is.

"All I do know is that our business will go down the drain and our insurance will go through the roof, and some of the companies might pull out if they think fraud is rampant in our county. And lord help us if we don't get this fixed before the next hurricane. We might never see an insurance agent again," Amos said.

The investigator thought for a moment, and Amos looked at his watch.

"It's gonna take time, and money," the investigator said.

"Well, you have very little of one, and an unlimited amount of the other," Amos said. "Get to work."

The investigator nodded, and sat in the little room, thinking of his next steps, until the Citation roared down the runway and disappeared into the southern sky.

On board the Citation, Amos smiled. That insurance speech was total bullshit.

If there was a guy behind all these fires, he didn't want to jail him.

He wanted to hire him.

Pauline hung her head as the door slammed shut. There were never easy answers in this job. Always problems, rarely solutions. A neighborhood's sewer was backed up, or the water line was broken. The trash people missed a street. The budget was off by ten percent. She needed new employees she couldn't find, or she had to fire someone because of a bad drug test. Somebody was always mad. Always slamming the door.

And now her beloved catamaran, her beloved retreat, needed repairs along with the dock where she moored it. She hadn't figured out where to move the boat, if anywhere, so when this miserable, frustrating day ended, her only option was home where her shit weasel of a husband was waiting to make her life more miserable.

She brought the meeting to a close and thanked everyone.

As they left the room, the local fire chief hung back and asked for a minute.

"There's something you need to know," the chief said. "I want to share it with you privately."

Pauline sat back down and said okay.

"This isn't about boats," the chief said. "You remember the fires at Bud Grant's rentals?"

"Yeah," Pauline said, "during the hurricane."

"That's right," continued the chief. "We did our investigation, and it sure looked like the wind blew a tree into the power line that went to one of the houses and the wind spread it to the others. What was interesting was how fast it spread, even with the high winds."

"Bud's insurance company paid a crew to clean up the debris and haul it away. They found something and called us," the chief said.

Pauline leaned forward. "What?" she asked.

"We think it was a firebomb."

Pauline looked at him in disbelief. "A firebomb?"

"Yes, ma'am. It was a plastic drink bottle filled with some sort of fuel and had a timer attached to it. For some reason it didn't detonate and didn't burn up in the fire."

Pauline was captivated, but also pissed.

"Why am I just now hearing about this?" she demanded.

"Well, ma'am, we didn't exactly know how to handle the

news about it, so we kept it a secret. Weren't sure how the community would react. We brought in the bomb squad from the air force base, and they blew it up."

Pauline was growing more incredulous.

"I can't believe I haven't heard anything about this," she said, her face turning red. "I'm really disappointed, and we'll need to talk about how you handled this, but the larger issue is that a firebomb was found in a burned-out rental place. Do you think the rest of the houses were torched?"

"I can't prove it," the chief said, "but my gut says yes. That little bomb is our only evidence. The houses burned clean. There was no smell of gas or any other sign of arson."

"So, what do we do?" Pauline asked.

"No clue," the chief said.

VI. THE PRIVATE EYE

The private investigator was completely flummoxed, maybe for the first time in his career.

He had been up and down the coast, to all the marinas where boats had burned. He found what was left of some of the roasted and toasted little boats, and he realized that it doesn't take long in the salt water and sea air for the rust and corrosion to wipe away clues and secrets about what had happened.

Nobody was talking, either. He pretended to be an insurance adjuster, then an insurance investigator, then lied about being a state investigator. He was able to track down a handful of aspiring sea captains whose boats were destroyed by fire, but they had nothing to say. They had their insurance checks and probably had already spent them on something else they couldn't afford.

There were some claims for cars that were burned, but

there weren't that many, and this seemed to be a boat issue, at least to him.

He did some background checking to see if only one or two insurance companies were involved. But, based on what he could find, it looked like dozens of companies insured the destroyed boats, so there was no trend there that helped point him in any useful direction.

He was running out of ideas, so he dropped by the local newspaper office and asked to thumb through their recent editions.

It was a typical local paper. He flipped through page after page of stories about the controversies over new neighborhoods, street pavings, pageant winners, and softball scores. He was about to consider this a dead end also when he turned the page to the little paper's coverage of the hurricane which had roared through a month earlier.

He was actually impressed. The quality of the stories and the photographs, in his mind, were probably award-winning as the paper's skeleton staff did a very thorough job of documenting the worst thing that had happened to their community in a decade.

There was breathtaking coverage of escapes from collapsed houses, rescues of people swept away by swift water, and boats being flung onto the shore by the high waves.

And then a story about a massive fire that erupted during the storm.

He read it, then read it again.

He thought, *it seems odd that such a fire could happen during a torrential downpour in a hurricane.* Of course, the winds could've pushed it along. Something didn't make sense to him. The story said a tree limb knocked a power line loose. He wondered when the power went out, and if this is really what caused the fire. The power always goes out in a hurricane, it's just a matter of when.

He leaned back in his chair and thought for a moment. He had not always been a private investigator. Like many folks in his field, he'd been a cop and later a detective, so he was suspicious of everyone and everything and rarely believed anything he saw or heard.

Something wasn't right, and he couldn't explain it. But he had nothing else.

He tracked down the address where the big fire occurred and drove out there that afternoon, parking at the top of the gravel drive. There was nothing special to see, just the smudged foundations of the five houses, some leftover debris here and there. He was officially trespassing, but he had plenty of fake IDs if he needed them.

He walked around the perimeter of the lot, looking at the trees and the remaining utility pole that likely had provided power to the homes. It was scorched from the fire, but he didn't see anything that was helpful.

"Whatcha looking for, mister?"

He turned, and there was a kid, maybe a teenager, on a bike. He'd snuck up on him. How'd that happen?

"You looking for something?" the kid asked.

"Um, no, just looking around. It's quite a mess," the private investigator said. "What are you doing here?"

"I live just over there," the kid said, sweeping his bony arm toward a row of trees.

"Did you see the fire?"

"I saw it from my house. My momma and daddy wouldn't let me out in the storm. But we could see it. It was huge! And we could smell it."

"I bet that was scary," the private eye said.

"Naw, it was cool."

Then the kid continued.

"I came over here and watched 'em bulldoze everything. That was totally cool. And while they're doing that, they stopped, and put up yellow tape like you see on tv, like when somebody's murdered."

"Oh really," the investigator said. "That does sound cool. What happened then?"

"Well, they quit for a while and didn't do nothing. I went home for lunch, and when I came back there was this crazy looking truck with blue and red lights flashing, and some guys like you see in the movies. They looked like ninjas to me!"

"You're kidding," said the investigator. "Go on."

"So, these guys put something–it wasn't very big–in the back of the truck, and moved over there," the kid said, pointing to an open area across the gravel drive from where the homes were. "There was a bang, and they opened the back door and smoke came out. Then they left."

This was an incredible story, the investigator thought, and there was no reason this kid was making this up, even though he was a little skeptical that the kid had just shown up and starting jabbering.

"Well, thanks, buddy, sounds like a neat adventure. I appreciate you telling me about it," he said.

"No problem, see ya," the kid said, and he pedaled off.

The ground rules of the interview had been agreed to and were in writing.

The magazine writer would be allowed onto the Air Force base and would be accompanied by the base's public affairs officer at all times. He would be allowed to interview two soldiers for forty-five minutes and couldn't identify them or be specific about any job they had done. No photographs. The base would provide him with some stock photos that had been approved for public use. His notebook would be reviewed at the conclusion.

The story was pitched as a breezy, feel-good piece about how the Air Force base's bomb squad occasionally responds to crises in local communities when they need help and don't have the right resources. It was usually a situation where the local cops or fire department find a suspicious bag or some crazy device with wires and a battery, and their first thought is that the Ayatollah has invaded their Podunk town to blow it up. The Air Force would dispatch its bomb squad, which had the technology and good sense to render the town safe from invading hordes.

On this day, the Air Force was interested in some good PR in the area after some recent drunk and disorderly behavior had local elected officials thinking about declaring the bars off limits to the airmen.

"Thanks for meeting with me," said the private investigator, who said he was from Coastal Resorts magazine and hoped that nobody would call them to verify until he got what he wanted.

Across from him was the public affairs officer and two staff sergeants who operated the bomb disposal unit. They reported to a lieutenant who wasn't available today.

The interview went well, and the sergeants were well prepared by their PR guy. They spoke easily of the important relationship between the base and local communities, and about how proud they were to respond when there was a crisis and how they were happy their skills could be put to good use. They told two approved stories of incidents where they helped, but no specifics.

As they wrapped up, the private investigator memorized the last names on the sergeant's uniforms. And, when he completed his debrief with public affairs officer, he returned to his car in the parking lot.

Across the lot, he saw the two sergeants he'd just interviewed under the hood of a pickup truck, trying to jump start it.

And he knew immediately that he'd found what he needed.

Staff sergeant Baker loved his F150, but it was trying his patience.

He was under the hood again, this time in his driveway,

trying to figure out what was wrong. He didn't want to trade it, even though every car dealer in the state had great deals for military customers.

He and his wife lived off base, in a neighborhood of tract houses that all looked alike and catered to the airmen and their families. It was a typical military neighborhood, where everyone huddled together and supported each other, especially when there were deployments.

He had replaced all the F150's key parts, but the battery wouldn't charge, and it sometimes cut off in traffic. He'd spent all his extra cash on it. His wife wouldn't drive it. He was beginning to worry it might not crank one day when he got paged to bomb squad duty. He just stared into the engine compartment, oily rag in one hand.

Then, a voice behind him.

"Hello, sergeant, remember me?"

Baker turned to see a stranger standing on the sidewalk, not yet in his yard.

"Uh," Baker said, staring at him coolly, trying to place the stranger.

"I'm from the magazine. We did the interview the other day."

"Oh yeah," Baker said. "What's up?"

"Can I come in your yard?"

Baker waved him forward.

The private investigator stepped on the driveway and moved toward the F150.

He had planned to tell the sergeant that he needed some

more details for his story, and that he'd promised that nobody would ever know they'd had an unauthorized conversation.

But he changed his mind.

"Listen, sergeant, I'm gonna be honest with you," he said. "I'm not a magazine writer."

"I figured that," Baker said. "Your questions were pretty lame."

"I'm a private investigator, and I've been hired to figure out all these boat fires around here," he said. "And then there were those houses that burned in the hurricane. I'm wondering if there was a connection, and I know you guys were there. Can you tell me what was going on?"

Baker looked at the ground and then back into this befuddling engine compartment. *How'd he know that?*

"You know I can't, or I shouldn't," Baker said.

"Honey, is everything okay?" came a shout from the house when his wife noticed a stranger in their driveway.

"Yes, everything's good," he yelled back.

The private investigator looked at him, trying to figure if there was an opening, and decided to go for it.

"We can get this thing fixed," he said, nodding toward the truck. "I just need a little something to go on."

Baker leaned against the truck, and after a minute of thinking about it, crossed the line.

"It was like a little pipe bomb," he said, looking at the ground. "It was a plastic Gatorade bottle with a timer. We didn't examine the contents, thought it was too volatile, but we didn't know for sure. It was so small we just decided to detonate it and move on."

Holy shit, thought the investigator. Those houses were indeed torched.

"There's more," the sergeant said.

"Is it worth a new truck?"

"You decide."

"Okay, tell me."

"There was a fingerprint."

The private eye just looked at him.

"The state boys pulled it off the Gatorade bottle while we were there. Asked us if we needed a copy for our files. I said sure. They sent me a copy later."

"You have it?"

"Yep."

"Can I have it?"

"Yep."

"Let's go to the dealership."

VII. FLORIDA

The Pelican Inn was a throwback, a long throwback, to a different era.

It was two stories and had thirty apartments in an "L" shape that wrapped around a pool and a cabana. The Pelican took up a city block in the suburb called Lauderdale by the Sea and was the winter getaway for Canadians and snowbirds who migrated to Florida every winter to escape the misery of a northern winter.

The Pelican Inn had existed since before Lauderdale by the Sea had an official name, and for many years stood alone in this neighborhood. Now it was surrounded by enormous pink, green, and white sky-scraping condos which loomed over the little Pelican from all sides. Dozens of offers had come in over the years, all of them in the tens of millions of dollars, for the land where the Pelican sat so it could be torn down and replaced by another sky-scraping condo.

Marian had always said no, and often didn't respond at all, even when one offer was accompanied by a threat of physical harm to Marian and her guests. She shrugged off such nonsense. She was tougher than any of them, and unafraid.

The Pelican Inn remained what it was because Marian promised her father on his death bed that his creation and vision would never change and absolutely never be sold while she was alive.

So, now the wonderful anachronism lived on, empty for most of the summer until the regulars started to trickle in when the weather turned cold up north. The same folks returned every winter; some were second and third generation. Marian never increased their rent, so whatever they paid the first year they stayed at the Pelican became their rent forever.

Marian was a large, gregarious woman, a loud talker and wonderful storyteller. One of the reasons her guests always returned was the evening poolside cocktail party over which she presided and for which no one ever received a bill. It was a marvelous gathering every night at dusk, with cool Florida drinks, tall tales, occasional live music, but always the center of attention was Marian and her collection of nonsense and stories, waving her flabby wing-like arms at the surrounding, lurking intimidating condos and telling them all to go to hell.

Jeff was now a part of this world.

He and Mira had fled here because Mira's Aunt Marian had said they could. Marian was pleased and relieved that Mira was back in her life and had promised she wouldn't be so hard on her this time. Marian offered them an apartment that needed renovating before it could be rented this winter, and assumed they were a couple and would be happy to share. But they weren't a couple. There was nothing sexual or physical between them; in fact, the only time he'd touched her was when he dragged her to his truck to escape the tornado, and nothing since. They relied on each other, but for nothing more than survival.

Marian needed a handyman, so that was Jeff's new job. He did the job for a place to stay, and he was good. Marian's previous handyman was her pitifully henpecked husband who had died a couple of years ago, and nobody including Jeff would ever do things the way her late husband did. But Jeff did better than the others. And, in the evenings when his chores and odd jobs were done, Marian always made him feel welcome at the poolside parties, and he usually went.

After a month, Mira was gone.

Neither Jeff nor Marian were really surprised. Jeff had no idea where to look for her, so he didn't. He assumed she had returned to her old life there in Florida, in the deep, dark hole where drug addicts always return, even though they promise they won't, a hole they can never escape.

Life at the Pelican moved on without her. Autumn was approaching, and familiar faces would soon be there.

Amos Andrews had everything. His investments and properties were pouring in so much cash that it was difficult to manage. Of course, owning a Citation is an excellent way to get rid of cash in a hurry when a tank of gas costs five grand and a million for its annual inspection and service.

He had no personal life, no time for it or need for it. The cougars and widows in the low country and Southport were always stalking him, hoping to lure him into their clutches so they could enjoy his lifestyle and stick their manicured fingers into his pocketbook. He often wondered why he avoided having a woman in his life. He didn't think he was gay; no, that wasn't it. He finally concluded they were more trouble than they were worth and enjoyed the flexibility and thrill of ordering up the Citation for a quick trip somewhere without coordinating around somebody's hair appointment.

But, today, none of his money or jets or anything could fix his problem.

He was beyond mad. He seethed with such anger that his brain was in a fog.

He had flown back last night from Southport after a week of reviewing his properties and checking on the books with the accountants. He had landed at dusk, and it was completely dark when he returned to his gated community, to his elegant home that overlooked the river that flowed lazily through the property and provided spectacular scenery for a few of the best homes and several of the best golf holes.

He was satisfied with his life and with how his businesses were performing in Southport. He slept later than usual and was a happy man.

Until he threw open the drapes of his bedroom window to enjoy the magnificent view of the early-morning low country sun rising over the river.

What he saw made him nauseous. And then angry. Trembling anger.

In his neighbor's yard, every palm tree, every pine tree, every bush, anything that had a root, was gone, all the way down to the river's edge. Nothing but raw, gray dirt, with a few helpless shoots of leftover vegetation randomly poking up out of the ground.

His neighbor, a despised, arrogant doctor, was preparing to build an estate next door, and Amos knew that the construction would be a pain and a nuisance.

But nothing like this. The neighborhood association and the local government had strict rules about tree and vegetation removal, and he knew you absolutely couldn't uproot everything because he'd butted heads with them while building his house, and he learned about the rules the hard way with a five-thousand dollar fine when he removed a single palm tree without permission.

He got on the phone with the club manager.

"What in the hell is going on at Doc Peterson's place," he demanded.

"I have no idea, but I'm on my way," the club manager replied and hung up.

They met on Peterson's lot, and walked on the barren soil down to the edge of the river, where nothing was left except a new, small gully that had washed a trail of filthy gray silt into the river. Peterson's new estate now had an unobstructed view of the river, a view enjoyed by no one else because no one else dared violate the rules in such an indecent way. Where there had been twenty-five mature pine trees, there were now none, unless you counted the twenty-five stumps.

"What an asshole," the manager said. "He never asked for the club's permission for this, he just did it. He knew he couldn't get what he wanted playing by the rules, so he just did it."

"So what can be done?" Amos asked. "He can't get away with this. If he does, what's to stop the next asshole who's not afraid to be the next asshole?"

"Mr. Andrews, this is a mess," the manager replied.

So, the neighborhood association called in Doc Peterson and yelled at him and pointed out all the rules he'd broken. He feigned ignorance of some of the rules and alleged that he didn't realize he'd needed some paperwork.

But the neighborhood association members overheard Peterson smugly bragging at the club that there was nothing anyone could do to him, and he now had a better view of the river, and nothing the club or the town did to him could cause his view to ever be obstructed like it was before he bulldozed the place.

So the neighborhood association fined him, and the club suspended him, but they knew he was laughing at them because he was right. He got what he wanted, and they couldn't undo it. The town levied a civil penalty of ten thousand dollars, but he laughed at that also. Both the neighborhood and town were requiring him to replace trees and bushes, and he laughed at that as well.

Amos was one of those who overheard Doc bragging about his misdeeds, and it infuriated him so much that he sat his unfinished drink on the bar and left. *I don't want to be in a club with an asshole like that, and no asshole like that should get to live in our neighborhood.*

So, with every nail that was driven, every load of lumber that was delivered, and every pipe that was laid on Doc's new place, it incensed Amos to the point that his anger was causing him to lose sleep and actually think about moving somewhere else. *But why should I be the one to pay the price?*

His mind kept roiling, and then he thought of a solution.

The wreck, by Florida standards, was pretty minor.

Jeff was in Marian's old van, on the way to pick up supplies. He'd sold his own truck when he got to Florida, just to put in an extra step if anyone was looking for him.

It was late afternoon, and he ran a stop sign as he cut through an unfamiliar neighborhood to avoid the usual lockdown on I-95. He tee-boned an ancient Cadillac whose octogenarian driver wasn't wearing a seat belt because it infringed on his constitutional rights, so the impact bounced the old guy around pretty good. Jeff went to him immediately and could tell he wasn't really hurt but putting on a good show when the paramedics arrived.

It was clearly his fault, so the cops charged him. At that time of day, everyone under the age of a hundred in Florida is assumed to be drunk if they cause a wreck like this, so they took him in for the obligatory breathalyzer and to Jeff's horror, fingerprinting. His North Carolina driver's license had expired, so they wrote him up for that. He wasn't drunk, obviously, and resisted the fingerprinting so furiously that the cops looked at each other and wondered what he was guilty of. They mentioned it to their supervisor, who promised them he'd pop Jeff's prints on the national database first chance he got.

Jeff was more traumatized by the fingerprinting than by destroying an old van belonging to Marian, who was only frustrated that her insurance was probably going up.

The police captain in the tiny town of Belhaven was a captain of no one.

He was the town's only cop, so that made him the chief as well. He'd never understood why the town council didn't make him chief, and why they thought it was fair and decent to pay a man only twenty-five thousand dollars a year to be the thinnest blue line that ever existed.

He was the only one to answer the calls for break-ins, fender benders, and barking dogs no matter the time of day or night. He could get help from deputy sheriffs if he needed it, but sometimes they were a half-hour away. And the town expected him to hang out at the town's edge where the speed limit dropped abruptly to twenty-five miles an hour and generate revenue by sticking it to the transient vacationers who didn't pay attention.

His cruiser was junk, bought at a state auction after the highway patrol had beat it nearly to death. His uniform was stained and worn, his taser battery expired two years ago, and he was behind in his required firearms training.

He did get a free lunch every day at the cafe on the main street, so that was something. He was eating hamburger steak and gravy when a citizen asked if he could join him. He said sure.

"I'm sorry to bother you," said Amos Andrews' private investigator, "but I couldn't find the police station and I saw your car out front. I hope this is okay."

"I don't mind. What can I do for you?" the captain replied.

The private investigator handed a business card, made specially for this occasion. He explained that he owned a company that was developing a technology to help law enforcement quickly analyze data, like DNA and fingerprints.

"The challenge I have," the private investigator said, "is testing it in the field to see if it really works. The big-city police departments blow me off because they don't have time. And I don't mean to insult you, but I thought you might have time."

The captain swallowed the rest of his hamburger steak, and looked at his radio, which had remained silent throughout lunch.

"Well, I don't know. I suppose we, or I guess I, could help, as long as it doesn't interfere with police business," the captain said. "What exactly do you need?"

The private investigator said all he needed was access to the captain's computer system that would allow him to search for fingerprints. Maybe an hour a day for a couple of weeks. The going rate was a thousand an hour, paid once a week in cash, and it would take about twenty days.

The captain did the math quickly in his head.

"Do you do business with me, or does this have to go through the town," he asked.

"Any way you want it," said the private eye, knowing the answer.

"I'll be glad to help," said the captain. "You can work with me."

Bud left the meeting with the fire chief more shaken than ever. The chief was determined to find who'd torched Bud's houses, but he was running into obstacles everywhere as he tried to match the fingerprint on the little bomb with the various data bases.

He had asked Bud to stop by the fire station to see if he could help.

"Nothing but dead ends," he told Bud, sitting on the front bumper of Engine One. "The state investigators don't return my calls, and I don't have the equipment to compare the print I've got with those on the computer system."

Bud thought for a minute and wasn't eager at all to offer his services.

"Bud, I need some help," the chief continued. "This is one of the worst things ever to happen in this community. It looks bad on me that I can't solve it. The county manager is yelling at me, Amos Andrews is yelling at me, and I've got no plan and no idea on what to do next."

Bud kept hoping his radio would summon him to some highway catastrophe and save him from this conversation.

"Yep, it can be frustrating," he told the chief. "But I don't have access to any of those records, either." He continued. "Chief, let's be honest. I got my insurance money, so I'm good. Why don't you let it go?"

"No way," the chief said, standing up from his seat on the bumper. "This is a crime in our town. Somebody did this deliberately. And I'm gonna keep searching till I find the bastard, and I'll call in all the help I can find."

Bud said he needed to go and headed to his cruiser, a desperate plan developing in his mind.

He called his rental agent, and they agreed to meet.

"We've gotta do something," Bud told the agent. "I can't live like this."

He described his conversation with the fire chief and told the agent he was terrified that the chief would continue digging and probing until somebody finally talked.

"Well, that somebody won't be me," the agent said. "And why are we even talking?"

"Because you're in this up to your ass," Bud said. "You were the deal maker! You paid him the money, not me! What about your so-called associate who made the delivery to the Crazy Crab, or the bartender? I bet he knows too much if the right person asks the right question or scares him to death," Bud said.

"They don't know enough," the agent said. "Even if they got questioned, they wouldn't be any help and, besides, they would never go to jail for what they did, so no worries there." He continued. "The fingerprint is the problem. Which means the only person we need to worry about is the dude who did the deed."

"I have an idea," Bud said.

He explained his plan to the agent.

"So let me get the straight," the agent said after listening in disbelief to what Bud described. "We're moving from a simple little arson to a conspiracy to commit murder? And you're a state trooper who we entrust our lives with? Have you lost your mind?

The agent was reacting to one of the craziest things he'd ever heard.

Bud proposed to track down the arsonist wherever he was and "take care of him." It all hinged on whether his contacts who were state investigators could match the fingerprint and if that match led him to the arsonist, whom he would then stalk until he could implement, as he said, "a permanent solution to the threat."

"I'm out," the agent said. "This whole thing has messed up your head. There's no threat. Nobody's gonna find this guy. He committed a major crime. He's gone underground. You need to get back to harassing speeders and quit this nonsense."

"Then," Bud said, "I'll do it without you."

VIII. LOW COUNTRY

MARIAN'S DUSK soirée was in high gear.

It was a beautiful early winter evening in Florida, the perfect temperature that made everyone pleased that they were here and not shoveling snow back home. Marian was more boisterous than usual, and all the residents of the Pelican Inn were enthralled with her latest loud tale of some adventure from her maidenhood that was preposterous and hysterical. Everyone was laughing and drinking.

Jeff was sitting at the cabana after a long day of doing Marian's chores and enjoying a free beer. He had heard all of Marian's stories by now, so he wasn't listening and really wasn't paying attention to anything.

"Are you Jeff?" asked a voice. "Actually, I know you are."

Jeff turned toward a stranger.

"You're a hard man to find," Amos Andrews said.

Jeff looked at him and didn't reply immediately.

Finally he said, "I'd have tried harder to not be found if I'd known somebody was looking."

"Well, Jeff, a lot of people are looking for you," Amos said. "You're actually lucky I'm the one who did."

"You've got one minute to tell me what this is about," Jeff said, standing up from his stool at the cabana bar.

"It's gonna take longer than a minute," Amos said, "and I don't think you're in a position to make many demands."

It took almost an hour, but Amos laid it all out. He was unafraid to tell Jeff the details of how he arrived at Marian's little party.

He told him how he had a private investigator working for weeks to figure out who was burning all the boats along the North Carolina coast, and in particular who had been responsible for the fire at his marina. Nobody believed the story about a malfunctioning bilge pump, but nobody could prove anything different.

Amos said his instincts were that someone was behind all those fires, someone who was professional and clever and thorough and would never be caught unless he made a mistake.

Like the mistake Jeff had made.

Amos told Jeff a story he already knew, about the unexploded gator bomb and the fingerprint the authorities found. Jeff's mind flashed back to that terrifying night that was unlike anything he'd lived through, and how distracted he'd been when he found Mira in the abandoned house, and not setting the final bomb properly. And how finding her and saving her might be costly for him.

"Are you the law?" Jeff finally asked.

"No," Amos replied, smiling.

He told Jeff the highlight version of how he'd gotten his fingerprint, and didn't feel the need to go into a lot of details about bribing Air Force sergeants and small-town police officers to get it. He did tell him how his private investigator had found a match in the national registry that was generated by a police report for a wreck in Fort Lauderdale. The cops who worked the wreck were happy to help when offered a couple of hundred- dollar gift cards to Ruth's Chris, and had some notes about where Jeff was staying even though his license was expired.

"So, here I am," Amos said. "I'm glad I found you."

"And if I've found you, others will, too," he continued. "The fire department in Southport has your fingerprint and access to the same database. They may not have the same incentives as my guy, however."

"Okay, so you're not the law, and you think you're clever and have things all figured out," Jeff said.

He continued, defiantly. "I don't know what you're talking about. That's my official answer, in case you're recording our conversation. I haven't done anything wrong. It's time for you to leave."

"That's fine," Amos said, "and I expected you to say something like this. But here's the deal. I've got a personal issue that's eating me alive. You're not in trouble with me. But I need your help."

Jeff said he'd listen, but not tonight, and not here. Tomorrow night, and I'll call you with the location.

Jeff called Amos and gave him the address of a little bar on the outskirts of Lauderdale by the Sea. When Amos arrived, Jeff wasn't there. The bar's hostess said she had a message from Jeff: *Meet him on the curb, and he'll pick you up.*

Very clever, thought Amos. *He suspects that I've set him up and tipped off others to where he'll be. Oh well, I'll play along.*

Jeff pulled up in Marian's new van, and Amos climbed in after looking into the back to make sure there were no ninjas or mobsters poised to attack him.

Jeff drove to the end of the block and parked at a city park. They got out and walked to a picnic table. The park was crowded, so neither of them could do anything stupid.

"Okay, here we are," Jeff said. "Let's have it."

Amos told him the story of his beautiful home on a river in low country South Carolina, and how the asshole next door had raped his yard and the shore of the river, broke all the rules and laws, and thumbed his nose at everyone who did the right thing. He said the riverside looked like a boxer's mouth with a front tooth missing where there was a gap caused by the asshole's destruction of every living thing along the river.

"What does this have to do with me?" Jeff asked.

"I have a business proposition for you," Amos said.

"I'm retired," Jeff replied. "I'm a professional handyman who drives a van belonging to the aunt of a missing woman whose life I saved. That's who I am."

"I understand," Amos said. "I want to hire you. It can be your last job ever."

Jeff said nothing. So, Amos continued.

“What I need,” Amos told him, “is to make that asshole's house go away. With lots of drama.” His voice trembled in anger. "He can't get away with what he did, and there's nothing that anyone can do to make him pay for what he did. It's simply wrong."

Amos went on. "Everybody hates him for what he did. Several people said they'd kill him, but they don't mean it. And then one person, who's one of the sweetest ladies I know, said she'd love to burn down the place. That's where I got the idea."

"So," Amos said. "There it is. When the construction on his house is just about complete, I want it gone just like those five houses in Southport and whatever else you burned. No trace, and impossible to figure out what happened. Just a pile of ashes. I want him to be so devastated that he leaves, and we never see his face again.

"But this time," Amos added, "make sure all the bombs go off. We don't need any duds laying around. Your fee is a hundred grand cash. Half tomorrow if you agree, the other half when the asshole's beloved mansion is a pile of smoking debris."

Jeff thought for a moment.

"Two hundred," he said. "Half tomorrow. And a promise that you'll help me disappear. I can't live worrying about anyone else finding me."

"Deal," Amos said. "You'll have the cash before the end of the day tomorrow. Have your plan ready then."

Four months passed, and Jeff didn't hear from Amos. He had been paid the hundred thousand as promised, so he was actually unconcerned about whether he ever heard from him again.

He had all the supplies he needed. He had two dozen Gatorade bottles, but he couldn't stand the taste of Gatorade, so he dumped the yellow mess down the drain and washed out the bottles, leaving off the caps so they'd dry out. He'd gotten the M80s from a shady source, so he went out into the country to make sure they worked, and they did.

But he couldn't figure out the jet fuel. He thought about all the different options, but they were all too risky. He decided he would simply be bold and go ask to buy some.

He went to the executive airport that served the corporate jets that flew into Fort Lauderdale and walked into the Banyan fixed based operations center with a ten-gallon fuel can. The young woman staffing the counter looked at him like was crazy.

"My plane ran out of gas," he said with a wry smile. "I walked here to get some."

She kind of snorted at the dumb joke and radioed the fuel truck operator to come to the front door. A minute later, the truck pulled up, and she pointed to the door as if to say, *there it is, go get you some.*

The truck's operator filled the can while chatting about the weather, and Jeff returned to the counter lugging the heavy can.

"That'll be fifty dollars, plus tax," she said. "You know it's five dollars a gallon."

He said that was okay, paid in cash, and headed back to the Pelican in a rented car.

When he got back, Amos had called.

"The bastard's house is nearly complete on the outside," he told Jeff. "They put the shingles on earlier this week and have started a lot of the carpentry on the inside. The asshole doctor was there yesterday with his whore girlfriend and a decorator picking out light fixtures and other stuff. They also stood on the deck and admired their wonderful view." Amos's voice was shaking.

"Anytime now is good," Amos said. "Once I give you the address, we won't speak anymore or meet until it's time for me to pay you. Is everything still good with you?"

Jeff said it was and that he'd rent a car and drive there this week. He told Amos that the next thing he knew, he would be getting awakened by his neighbor's house on fire.

They talked about one of the big logistical problems: access to a fancy gated community for an arsonist. They both laughed at the notion. The plan they came up with made them laugh also. Amos would call the front gate, pretend to be Doc Peterson, and get a gate pass for Jeff under the pretense that he was a finish carpenter doing work on Doc's house. They thought the irony was wonderful, and an elegantly simple solution.

Jeff arrived in the low country without incident, which was good since he was hauling jet fuel and the other ingredients for a dozen little bombs.

He went on a reconnaissance mission to check out the target, and immediately there was a problem. His name wasn't at the front gate, and the security guys said they weren't allowed to disclose whether a Dr. Peterson lived there or not. Jeff turned away, confused and frustrated and unsure what to do.

He waited a few minutes, then tailgated a car through the members-only gate and sped into the neighborhood before the security boys could see him.

He wandered around the neighborhood, but nothing made any sense. He couldn't find the right street, and he didn't see anything under construction or any disgraceful tree removal that had started all this. He didn't see a river, either. He finally found a street that sounded like the one Amos had given him—maybe he'd misunderstood Amos—and followed it slowly until he found the right house number. But it still didn't look right. This house was either finished or not under construction at all. And it had plenty of trees. He needed to get this straightened out before he bombed anything.

He escaped the neighborhood, returned to his hotel out on the interstate, and phoned Amos.

Amos was irritated by the call because this was the mark of an amateur, and he thought he'd hired a pro.

But as they compared notes and tried to figure out what happened, it became clear. Every neighborhood in the area was named Palmetto Something: Palmetto Bluff, Palmetto Sands, Palmetto Landing, Palmetto Whatever. And every street sounded the same: Ocean View, River Landing, Soundside Drive. How the fire department ever found the right house was a miracle.

They finally concluded that Jeff was at the wrong Palmetto

Whatever, and Amos helped sort that out, so Jeff was exactly clear on which Palmetto he was going to.

He arrived later that afternoon at the correct Palmetto, and the security guard had his name but grilled him on why he was showing up at a job site so late in the day. Jeff wasn't prepared for this and bluffed his way by telling the guard he was setting up for his guys to go to work first thing in the morning. That satisfied the guard, more or less, and he scowled at Jeff as he opened the gate.

Jeff found the doctor's house and also admired Amos's place. *Very nice,* he thought. He also was stunned at the gap in the tree line by the river and didn't blame Amos at all for how he felt. A truck from the gas company was in the doctor's unfinished driveway. *Maybe they're turning on the gas,* he thought.

Jeff's plan was to find a secluded spot to park for the next eight hours, but that would be tough with roving security guards, so he was probably better off to keep moving every so often. When he was fairly certain all the workers had left the doctor's house, he dropped off his igloo coolers and hid them in the garage, then left quickly. He would walk back when the time was right.

The hours moved slowly, and it seemed like it took forever to get dark, but he couldn't afford to be impatient. These things always work best in the darkest and loneliest hours of the night.

He stopped and dozed briefly, and awoke with a start when a car approached, but it wasn't security and it disappeared into the night. He thought about how dark it was, and how few streetlights there were.

He remembered another dark night, and the eerie sensation

when the flickering of flames replaced the darkness, and the world became alive and vibrant. He was prepared for that experience on this night.

Finally, it was two o'clock. He'd seen no cars for several hours and wondered if security patrolled all night. Surely, they do, and surely, they have no idea of how busy they'll be shortly.

He parked two blocks away on an undeveloped cul de sac. He had rehearsed his departure route from this location several times; nothing would be worse than to get tangled up and lost in the winding and confusing streets of a subdivision after unleashing hell.

His path to the house was completely dark; no streetlights were between him and the target. He slipped along the streets lined with magnificent homes and wondered what they'd think when their sleep is disrupted in a few minutes.

Jeff arrived at the doctor's house and looked around carefully. Everything was completely dark. He looked over at Amos's house. No lights on.

His coolers were where he'd left them. He assembled the bombs earlier, so all he had to do was put them around the house, set the timers, and flee.

Then, he heard something.

It was a giggle, perhaps, then he saw an orangish glow.

He peered through the darkness and watched as the glow moved back and forth.

Oh shit, he thought, not again.

He moved closer to the sound and the orange glow.

It was kids, smoking pot. On the back porch of the unfinished house.

They were passing the joint back and forth, enjoying the buzz, talking quietly and stifling their laughs.

He thought about clearing his throat, and startling them, hoping they'd run away. But part of the ruse of this bombing was it would be a construction accident, so those kids didn't need to know anyone was there late at night.

Jeff decided to wait them out. Surely, they'd leave when the pot ran out, and they did.

He watched them through the darkness as they weaved their way clumsily down the unfinished and unpaved driveway and disappear back to the homes of their wealthy parents who had no idea they weren't asleep in their beds.

Jeff moved quickly through the house. He had twice as many bombs as he needed, but Amos wanted this place vaporized into oblivion.

He thought about how every situation was different, how some houses or boats had souls and others didn't. He could always tell where there was love and where there wasn't, and this elegant never-to-be mansion had zero soul. He could tell, even in the darkness, that it was just a showplace for an asshole egomaniac rule breaker who was just a few minutes away from having a very bad night.

Jeff set the earliest timers for twenty minutes, and he double-checked every timer to make sure of no mistakes. He also wore rubber gloves. Lessons learned. He found the gas turnoff valve and twisted it. It hissed and smelled like rotten eggs, so the gas was definitely on. He opened the valve all the way and let it hiss. Clearly a construction accident.

He set the final timer and left, moving quickly two houses

down. He wanted to stay close enough so he could see what happened, then get to his car and leave.

Nothing happened. Maybe he'd lost track of the time and had moved faster than he thought.

Still nothing happened. The night remained dark and quiet. Was something wrong?

Suddenly a pop, then an explosion that turned dark night into day, with a concussion that nearly knocked him down even two houses away. Burglar alarms at three houses started blaring.

The doctor's house was gone, blown completely to pieces, nothing but a burning mess of rubble. Burning pieces of wood and roofing and everything else had been hurled in every direction, setting fire to the woods between the big houses. It looked like the roof of Amos's house might be on fire. Lights were on inside the house. *Good*, Jeff thought, *at least he's awake*.

As he scrambled to his car, off in the distance, the urgent sound of sirens.

Jeff was on his hands and knees in his motel room on the interstate, holding his head in his hands. He sobbed desperately and rocked back and forth, banging his head on the floor with each rock.

He rolled over on his back, his eyes squeezed shut, feeling like his head would explode.

How did this happen?

He finally turned off the tv as the early morning news show

kept blaring the news:

Two Bodies Found in Gas Explosion.

A low country tv station had a helicopter hovering over the site that had been Doc Peterson's mansion under construction. It was still smoking. The tv cameras on the ground showed debris throughout the neighborhood, with interviews with fire officials who confirmed that the natural gas had been turned on that day and something bad must've happened. No identities on the bodies found and no idea why they were in a construction zone at that time of night.

Jeff couldn't bear the thought that he was responsible for more death. Even if it was collateral, it was still on him. He tried to console himself that all this was because a rich man had a silly, petty gripe with a neighbor who was an even richer man. Rich people spending big money to settle stupid scores, and now somebody is dead. A couple of unfortunate families are getting devastating news this morning, and Jeff's finger was on the trigger.

He asked himself again. How did this happen?

There were obviously some kids there smoking weed, but he waited until he saw them leave, and he was certain they didn't return. Was someone else hiding in the house? How could that be? He was in every room, and even though it was dark, he was sure that he would have detected a couple of people. And when they saw him, why didn't they flee? Surely they knew he was up to no good.

How did this happen?

He lay motionless on the filthy carpet of the interstate motel, trying to gather his wits so he could make the long journey back to the Pelican Inn. He was finally composed enough to leave and opened the door that overlooked the parking lot.

He saw his rental car across the lot, blocked in by the cars of two sheriff's deputies. The deputies were looking at the car, not the motel.

He ducked around the corner and out of sight and ran across the access road to another roadside motel. He didn't have many good options, and nowhere to go. He tossed the rental car keys in a trash can as he entered the lobby, and rented a room with cash, just as he'd done across the street.

He then dialed 911 and reported that his rental car had been stolen.

A cop arrived in minutes, probably one of those at his car. Jeff told him all the rental paperwork was the in the car, and that he always left the keys to a rental car over the visor. The cop looked at him with one eyebrow raised, seriously not believing him.

The cop told them they had recovered the car, and it was just across the street. It was a suspicious vehicle but didn't tell him why. Jeff asked, said he had a right to know. The cop said the rental entered a gated community yesterday afternoon, and was videoed leaving at three am, just after a house blew up. They're checking all leads, the cop said.

"Can I have the car?" Jeff asked, "I need to return home."

"No way, mister, it's evidence."

Amos picked him up forty-five minutes later and went straight to the little airport that served the low country area. The Citation was parked outside the tiny terminal building, but it wasn't ready yet since the pilots didn't know they were flying today and had all the pre-flight stuff to do.

Amos and Jeff sat in the car, waiting for the pilots to give them a thumbs up.

"This is the best way to get you out of here," Amos said. "They'll never find you once you're gone."

Jeff said nothing.

Amos asked, "So, any idea of what happened? By the way, my roof has gotta be replaced."

Jeff went over the story again, about the teens smoking dope on the back porch and how he saw nobody else, and how he took advantage of the newly hooked up gas service to ensure the devastation was complete.

Amos shook his head. "I gotta admit, it was complete. I thought a plane had crashed. When you described your little bombs, I thought they'd just pop and start a fire, not an explosion like a nuclear warhead."

Amos continued. "We're in this thing deep, and there were serious, deadly consequences. I gotta know you're okay and not gonna melt down and say the wrong things to the wrong people."

One of the pilots walked to the car and gave a thumbs up. They could hear the Citation's engines spooling up.

"I'll be okay," Jeff said. "Just seems like everything I touch has...what did you call it, 'deadly consequences'."

IX. SNEAKERS

Amos hung around Fort Lauderdale for a few days after dropping Jeff at the Pelican. He stayed at the Westin and checked on Jeff's mental health a couple of times a day. Jeff seemed fine.

On the way to the airport for the quick Citation trip home, Amos came again to Jeff's small apartment at the Pelican.

He slid the bundles of the remaining cash he owed Jeff across the tiny dining table. As Jeff reached for it, he pulled the bundles back slightly, his hand still on them.

"I have another business proposition," he said.

Jeff just looked at him. "I'm retired, I mean really retired," he said.

"At least listen," Amos said, his hand still on the bundle.

Amos revisited the complicated and expensive effort to find him, and how it had been worth every penny. He was relieved to find Jeff, and startled to find that a place like the Pelican still existed, a relic of a different era in hospitality and surrounded by high rises with condos that sold for multi millions each.

Amos told Jeff that he'd done some checking and talked to a handful of the developers who had tried to buy the Pelican from Marian, and how she resisted all their charms and enormous sums of money. She told them all she'd made a promise to her father on his deathbed that the Pelican would stay like it was until she died, or something happened to the Pelican.

After a couple of martinis, one developer told him that he'd finally reached a deal with Marian to have the right of first refusal if she ever decided to sell before she died. He gave her twenty thousand dollars for this right, and now all he could do wait and hope for something to happen to the Pelican.

"And that's where we come in," Amos said.

Jeff dropped his head, chin on his chest. He knew where this was going. He didn't love Marian, but he adored and respected her and thought the Pelican was a cool little joint and there was still a place in this world for it. In fact, the world needs more Pelicans.

"I'm retired," a despondent Jeff said.

Amos pushed the bundle toward him.

"No you're not."

Bud spent weeks trying to get some help from his state buddies. At first, they said there was no match for the fingerprint, then they buzzed him a few days later and said there was a hit from a wreck in Florida, Fort Lauderdale to be exact.

Bud took a short vacation and drove non-stop to Fort Lauderdale to get more information. He flashed his badge around at the police department enough that he finally found the cops who'd investigated the wreck. They were annoyed that they had to dig out the file, but they finally found it and shared reluctantly with Bud, who noted that the driver had an expired license from North Carolina and his last known address was a motel in a nearby suburb.

"There's a lot of interest in this guy," one of the cops said. "What's he, an axe murderer?"

The cops laughed, but Bud didn't.

"Whadya mean, a lot of interest?" he asked.

"There was another dude," the cops said, "who came here and wanted the same info. He didn't tell us why, and we didn't care."

Bud thought for a minute and wondered who that could be. He thought he was the first person to track down the arsonist.

He was still puzzled, but these cops couldn't help him anymore, so he thanked them and left, prepared for the long drive back home.

"I guess if he'd bought us a steak dinner, we'd have told him about the feds poking around," one of the cops said, laughing. "You only get so much information for free."

Amos returned in a few days and put a sheet of paper in front of Jeff, who had taken a break from replacing a toilet in one of the apartments. It was the original toilet, and the regular guest had protested the need to replace it. "I'm used to it, and love it," he said when Marian called him in Ottawa with the sad news. Nevertheless, there were no replacement parts anymore, so it was time for it to go.

The sheet of paper was a partnership agreement. Jeff would be one of three partners in a limited liability corporation that would buy the Pelican from Marian when she had no choice but to sell. The LLC would pay for the property and to remove the debris from the site after the Pelican was destroyed by fire, then flip the property to the developer with the highest bid. The flip could net the partners ten million each.

Jeff couldn't believe any of this. He couldn't believe he was being asked, or told, to do another job. He couldn't believe it was The Pelican and poor Marian, both of whom would pay the price for greed. This was worse, in Jeff's mind, than the pettiness of the fire at Doc Peterson's never-to-be home.

"The summer season in Florida was a few months away," Jeff said, and it had to be then when The Pelican was empty. They had to guarantee, absolutely guarantee, Marian's safety. "No more collateral damage," Jeff said, glaring into Amos's eyes.

In the coming months, Jeff's thoughts went back and forth about this awful plot to steal The Pelican from Marian. The job itself would be easy. Every room had a small gas heater that was rarely used, even though there were some chilly Florida nights when even the Canadians and Yankees needed to knock off the edge. It would certainly look like a heater malfunction that spread surprisingly fast.

Jeff was on his back under a bathroom sink replacing a drain stopper that didn't stop anymore.

Marian found him. "Somebody here to see you. Waiting by the cabana."

Jeff wrenched his way out of the tight spot and looked at the cabana. Two men in dark suits. *Shit*, he thought.

He slowly made his way to the cabana. They introduced themselves, but all he heard was "FBI" and then acknowledged his own identity when they asked.

"We're here because our colleagues in North Carolina have an unsolved arson on their hands," one of them said. "We thought you might be able to help."

"Why do you think that?" he asked.

"Because we have reason to believe your fingerprint was on one of the devices used to start the fire," the agent continued.

He added that a small bomb was found in the debris of a burned-out house. It had a print, and then was destroyed by a bomb squad.

"Can we take your prints?" the agent asked. "You're entitled to have an attorney present. We can go to the courthouse where there'd be law enforcement witnesses. Or we can do it here. We have a kit."

Jeff thought about his options, and he also thought about the precautions he'd taken many months ago after his wreck and the terrifying experience of having his fingerprints taken made him fearful that this day would eventually come.

He had concocted a mixture of a mild acid and a couple of other ingredients which he'd tested on the skin of a supermarket chicken breast. His early tests completely melted the chicken, boring a sizzling hole all the way through the breast, and he had to return to Publix for more chicken. He learned that it took only a pinpoint drop to be effective. He tried it on his right thumb, guessing that the print on the bomb was one of his thumbs but without knowing for certain.

The pain was breathtaking, but he did four pinpoint drops on each thumb. When they healed in about six weeks, it was nearly impossible to tell that he'd tampered with his thumbs but also impossible to tell if he'd altered or disguised his prints enough to fool the FBI, for goodness sakes. Now, he was getting ready to find out.

They fingerprinted him right there on the cabana bar, first the fingers on both hands, and then the thumbs. They ignored the results of the fingers, and took out a magnifying glass, comparing the thumb prints they'd just taken with a copy of a print they removed from a slim briefcase. They both looked, moving the magnifying glass back and forth, squinting at each, while Jeff washed off the ink in sink of the cabana's bar.

"Thank you for your time," said the lead agent without emotion, handing him a business card. "If you decide to move or change addresses, please advise us."

At that moment, Mira came around the corner of the cabana.

Jeff almost passed out.

"Uh, hi," he said with a shaky voice. "Where you'd come from?"

The agents looked at each other and could tell Jeff had suddenly become spooked.

"Who are you?" the lead agent asked.

"Mirabelle, but my friends call me Mira," she said.

Jeff was having a horrifying flashback to the night of the hurricane and the house fires. *My god,* he thought, *she's a witness to a major crime standing here in front of the F friggin' BI. Jeez, what on earth is she gonna say?*

The agents asked how she knew Jeff, and she made up a pretty good story that omitted the part about North Carolina, any fires or hurricanes, getting stoned on meth, and her being totally missing for the last few months until just this moment.

The lead agent said, "Thanks for speaking with us."

And then they left.

After he got what he needed from the cops in Fort Lauderdale and before he drove home, Bud rode around until he found The Pelican Inn, and was pretty amazed that such a place still existed and wondered how the arsonist had ended up there.

He returned a month later to Florida by air, connecting in Charlotte to make his movements as hard to follow as possible.

Bud landed in Miami, the first step in an elaborate plan to eliminate the arsonist. His complicated plan was to leave a credit card trail around Miami in such a way that made it appear he was in Miami for his entire visit, and no one could conclude that he had time to go to Lauderdale by the Sea.

He began by checking into the Embassy Suites near the Miami airport. The next step was to head to a strip club a few miles away that he had learned with delight was a front for hookers. He had also done some checking and learned that it was a convenient place to buy a firearm, which he planned to do. The price would be exorbitant, probably twice the going rate, but he couldn't fly with a gun and a pawn shop or gun shop would require identification and other pesky paperwork. For his task, this would be better.

It was four in the afternoon, a little early for the hooker business, and the parking lot at Sneakers Men's Club was virtually empty. He opened the door to a refreshing woosh of chilly air conditioning, passed the disinterested gaze of the front-door bouncer, and checked in with the club's front desk, laying down his credit card and opening a line of credit. He asked for the manager, who appeared in a few minutes and took him down a long hallway to a cramped office filled with papers and cardboard boxes and decorated with posters of nude women.

He felt like he was in a scene from *The Godfather*.

"I need some assistance," Bud said. "And I was assured by an associate that you specialized in meeting the needs I have and doing so with utmost discretion."

The manager, who was definitely out of mobster central casting, eyed him.

"We specialize in meeting needs," he said. But, he added, matter of fact, "You're a cop."

Even in civilian clothes, Bud couldn't hide. His high and tight haircut and overall posture and demeanor were dead giveaways.

There's no point in trying to dodge the issue with a guy like this.

"Yes, I'm a state trooper in North Carolina," Bud admitted. "But I have some business in Florida that's unrelated to my job. I have some issues, and I believe you can help."

"If it's girls, we can provide whatever you need," the manager said, smiling, "and I mean whatever."

"Well," Bud said with a smile, "I'm definitely interested in that. You might say it's one of my favorite sports. But I need something else."

"What would that be, and why do you think I can provide it?" the manager asked.

"I need a tool for the business I need to conduct," and pulled out of roll of hundred-dollar bills. "I was told you could help."

The manager rolled his office chair over to a cabinet and opened the double doors. Inside was a rack of handguns and a shelf of ammunition boxes. Bud pointed to a Glock that was the same as his service sidearm and one box of ammo.

"If those are all hundreds," the manager said, pointing to Bud's roll, "I'll take thirty. And I could care less about what you do, but what you just bought needs to disappear when you're done."

Bud nodded that he agreed. And, with that, the deal was done. Bud asked the manager to send his best girl to the VIP suite and told him he'd opened a line of credit at the front desk, bringing the first smile of the meeting to the manager's face.

Bud's plan was to fool around for a little while, and then slip out for his trip to Lauderdale By The Sea without closing his tab, which would make it appear that he was at Sneakers the whole time.

He finally escaped the clutches of one of the hottest hookers he'd ever seen (*I need to come to Miami more often*), promised he'd be right back and slipped out the front door, telling the bored bouncer that he'd be gone a while but would return. The bouncer looked bored, but he made sure the club's surveillance cameras snapped a photo of Bud and his car.

He pushed the rental car hard, but rush hour was starting in South Florida, which meant nobody was going anywhere fast.

His phone rang. It was an unfamiliar number.

"Mr. Grant?" the caller asked.

"Yes."

"This is the First Union Bank fraud division," the woman on the line said. "We've detected what appears to be fraudulent use of your Visa. We want to make sure everything is alright. We've suspended the card until we talk to you."

"What's the problem?" he asked.

"There are some very large charges from a suspicious business," the caller continued. "In fact, your card has reached its limit."

Bud gasped. The limit on that card was twenty thousand dollars!

"And the business," the fraud lady added, "is Sneakers Enterprises, which our records show is not a legitimate business recognized by the State of Florida. Even though your card hit the limit, they are continuing to post charges to it, even as we speak. We've cut it off, unless you tell me it's not fraud."

"No, that's fine," Bud said, trying to suppress is panic while figuring out what to do. "Let me straighten it out and call you back." He hung up.

He didn't know whether to continue on his mission or return to Sneakers to stop the pillaging of his credit card.

After an agonizing back and forth in his cluttered mind, he concluded the arsonist will have to wait until tomorrow, and he turned the rental car back toward Sneakers.

As he drove south, he called the club, and yelled at whoever answered the phone to stop the run on his card. She told him to hold for a minute, then the mobster who ran the place picked up the phone.

"What's the problem?" he asked in his most mobster tone of voice.

"You know the problem," Bud yelled. "Y'all are running up my tab and I'm not even there. There'll be hell to pay if you don't stop right now."

"Don't threaten me," the manager said, and hung up.

Bud tried to redial, but the line was busy.

He was furious, shaking with anger, and getting angrier and more frustrated by the minute as he sat in the never-ending traffic jam of south Florida. There was no telling what he would've been paying for if he hadn't cut off the card. Hell, he couldn't imagine what he was paying for, and he wasn't even there! Suddenly nothing was going according to plan.

As he inched his way back to Sneakers in the heavy traffic, a police car pulled in behind him, flipped on its blue and red lights, and tooted the siren.

Bud pulled over. *What now,* he thought.

Two cops got out, weapons drawn, pointed at Bud's head. Bud had never been on this end of the deal. Cars that were barely moving slowed even more to rubber neck the spectacle.

He rolled down the windows and put both hands on the wheel where they could be seen.

"Exit the vehicle, hands where we can see them," ordered the cop on the driver's side.

He did so and was ordered to lie on the sweltering pavement, which he did, and was handcuffed and then leaned against his car, and then told to sit, his back against the car, his hands twisted awkwardly behind him. While one cop held a weapon on him, the other searched the car. It didn't take long.

"Here it is!" he yelled, holding up Bud's newly purchased Glock.

The cop who was watching him said, "We got a call that the person driving this vehicle had an illegal weapon and was planning to use it to commit a crime. You better have some paperwork for this piece, which we know you don't, or this is gonna get ugly real fast."

Bud was speechless. The Sneakers manager had ratted him out. Probably in exchange for some mobster bullshit he needed from the cops. These guys were probably on the mobster's payroll, and he calls them when he needs some quick action. That's the only way they found him so easily.

But he was busted, and this was spiraling out of control, he thought in a panic. *If I don't get this tamped down quickly, I'll lose my job.*

His mind raced.

He couldn't tell these cops the truth about the gun or that mobster at the hooker club would have him roughed up or probably rubbed out. *Goodness gracious,* he thought, *I'm talking to myself in mobster talk.*

Finally, he turned awkwardly to the cops.

"Listen guys, I'm a cop, too. My badge is in my hotel room. I didn't bring it with me. Let's go there and I can prove it to you," he said.

The cop with the gun on him didn't look away, but his buddy came over.

"We already know you're a cop," he said. "When we punched your name in the laptop, that's what showed up. What the hell are you doing in Florida with an unregistered gun? You're just a little bit out of your jurisdiction."

Just then, one of those out-of-nowhere Florida rainstorms opened up, making the situation for Bud even more miserable as he got soaking wet while sitting on the steaming pavement next to his rental car.

"C'mon guys," he pleaded.

Then it occurred to him. Tell the truth.

"Guys, listen. I'm here to find the guy who burned down five houses I owned. He's a damned arsonist, and none of the so-called professionals in North Carolina can find him. They're gonna give up on me, after all I've done for them and turned my back when they're doing sixty in a forty-five."

"But," he continued with all the earnestness he could

muster, "I've found him, and I've come to get him. I can't arrest him, but somebody in Florida can. That's why I have the gun, cause I couldn't bring my service weapon on the airplane."

The cop who had the bead on Jeff's head returned his weapon to its holster, and then looked at his colleague, not knowing whether to believe this story or not, but it was so detailed and crazy he thought it might be true.

He took the cuffs off Bud.

"Go home," he said to Bud. "Leave this gun with us. We'll clean up on this end, but you need to get out of here and forget this. If there truly is an arsonist, nothing good is going to happen when you find him. Go home."

Bud was back in North Carolina before dark.

The plan was set for the destruction of The Pelican.

They chose a mid-week night in June when no guests would be there. Marian was scheduled to be at a family reunion in North Carolina. Jeff had agreed to cover for her.

No little bombs this time. Jeff had designed a clever way to trigger a fire in one of the heaters. And in a new twist, he would be on the property and appear to try to gallantly save the burning building when actually he would go to several of the rooms and unhook the gas lines so the gas would fill those apartments. Once it got going, it would do enough damage to condemn the entire place, and his rescue efforts would be futile.

Amos and the other partner were satisfied with the arrangements, and were pleased that a new tactic was being used after hearing of the near miss with the FBI.

Jeff then paused to gather his courage, and said, "I am taking all the risk here, and that's not fair."

Amos and the third partner looked at each other.

"If you have the cash to buy the remains of the Pelican, then you have cash to advance me a portion of my share," Jeff said. "And that's what I want. At least a day before I torch her."

Amos was agreeable and had to talk the other partner into it. They finally agreed that a one-million-dollar cash advance was fair, considering Jeff was the only partner the FBI was nosing around about.

They shook hands, and Jeff said once he got the money there would be no further conversation between them and they should stay away. Don't come by to watch her burn. Don't come by to watch her smolder. That's how most arsonists get caught. As usual, he told them the next information they received would be that The Pelican was destroyed in spite of heroic efforts by the property's handyman to save it.

On the day before the Pelican's scheduled demise, Jeff and Amos met at the little city park down the street. Jeff's money was in a large briefcase, which he opened but didn't count.

"I'm going back to South Carolina," Amos said. "I look forward to hearing what happens. Good luck."

Jeff left two packages at the front desk of The Pelican.

One was addressed to Marian, and enclosed was a half million dollars with a note saying goodbye, and to always fight to keep The Pelican alive. And watch out for Amos. He's bad.

The other was addressed to Amos and was in a simple envelope. It contained only a note: "Do it yourself, you gutless bastard."

Jeff bummed a ride from Marian's yard guy, whose twenty-five-year-old Chevy pickup was having carburetor issues. It stalled in the driveway, but got them to the UPS store, where Jeff dropped off a small box addressed to Alyson's parents. *I'm sorry for all the pain I caused. I know this doesn't replace her, but I hope it helps in some way*. A half million dollars was enclosed.

He then told Marian's yard guy to take him to the Avis place, where he was planning to buy a used rental car with cash and head to the Keys.

As the old truck pulled out onto Federal Highway, it stalled, coughing and lurching to a halt.

And then they heard the siren.

The official report said the battalion chief of the Fort Lauderdale Fire Department had been traveling at ninety miles an hour. This information came from the onboard computer of the battalion chief's Tahoe. He was responding to a Code 1 alarm of a fire at a local deli owned and operated by a beloved Italian family who was the chief's cousin and his wife. Fire trucks from three different stations were rolling fast and hard because those firefighters ate there all the time.

By the time the chief smashed into old Chevy pickup, the onboard computer said his speed had dropped to seventy-five miles per hour and his brakes had locked up. The Tahoe hit the truck on the driver's side, nearly bending it in half. Witnesses said the battalion chief had the green light and lights and sirens were on.

The impact hurled the pickup onto the sidewalk, barely missing several terrified pedestrians and the shiny aluminum cart of a sidewalk hot dog vendor.

The pickup had no airbags or seat belts. The yard guy was flung across the front seat into his passenger, and the two of them were crushed together against the inside of the passenger door.

As some good Samaritans moved cautiously toward the mangled pickup and its trapped passengers, a sizzling noise started softly and rapidly grew louder, and then a fiery explosion blew the cab apart as the crowd on the sidewalk screamed in horror.

The battalion commander wrestled his way out of the Tahoe, untangling himself from the airbags and the seatbelt, trying to find the siren switch which still wailed, and looked for his handheld radio to call for help, still stunned by what had just happened.

He groped around for the radio, which he couldn't find, but he heard it crackling somewhere in the crumpled Tahoe, and the voice of the dispatcher calling out the address of the Italian deli:

All units cancel. Code 12.

False alarm.

THE END

AUTHOR'S NOTES

Some of my faithful readers may recognize the first two parts of *Burnt*. They are adapted from the short story "Fire Bug" that appeared in my short story collection, "Vanessa."

This book is a complete work of fiction. It's all made up. Readers may catch a whiff of reality or familiarity with some of the places and incidents. But, as the famous authors say, any resemblance to an actual person or place is coincidental.

However, The Pelican Inn was an actual place in Lauderdale by the Sea, and I went there as a child. It was owned by the parents of my Aunt Marian Morton McAdams, and operated by her and my Uncle Burch McAdams (my mother's brother) for many years. It's been long gone, but I moved it into the present for this book. Marian was one of the truly great characters in my life, and I hope my fond depiction of her brings happy memories for her family and friends if they ever happen to read the book.

I sincerely apologize to the brave men and women of the U.S. Coast Guard for dragging them into this book. I was just telling a story, and simply got carried away. I have total respect for your dangerous and heroic work, and my family proudly displays my late father's shoulder patches and badges from his service as a Coastie. To atone for my writing sins, a portion of the proceeds from the sale of this book will be donated to the Coast Guard Foundation. If, as expected, there are no sales, the author will take care of the contribution.

As always, my gratitude goes to the first person who always lays eyes on whatever I write, my favorite editor, Lisa Piercy. Her honest opinions, thoughtful suggestions and attention to detail greatly enhance the things I write and the life I live.

My thanks also go to Nate McHenry, Kay McHenry, and Barbara Reining for reviewing early manuscripts and providing excellent advice, suggestions and reactions, all of which improved the book immensely. Barbara was greatly relieved when I reassured her that gator bombs were imaginary and not something with which I had any real-life experience.

I'm deeply grateful to Kimberly Daniels Taws, the owner of The Country Bookshop in Southern Pines, NC, for her guidance and encouragement of this naïve novice, and for her patient and unwavering support of local authors. Buy local!

I also cannot tell you how much it thrills me that one my most faithful readers, Anne Piercy, is always excited about whatever I'm writing and eager to get a copy in her hands. Her enthusiasm always makes me want to start a new one.

ABOUT THE AUTHOR

Gene Upchurch is a native of Durham, North Carolina and a graduate of the University of North Carolina at Chapel Hill.

He was a sportswriter before embarking on a 28-year career in public affairs, community relations, and legislative advocacy in the utility industry. He is a proud recipient of the Order of the Long Leaf Pine, the State of North Carolina's highest civilian honor.

His previous novel, *The Eno Club*, was not an international bestseller, nor was his collection of short stories, "Vanessa".

He lives in Pinehurst with this wife, Lisa, and their two Norwich Terriers, Shelby and Hootie.

www.ingramcontent.com/pod-product-compliance
Lightning Source LLC
Chambersburg PA
CBHW010448310726
48979CB00018B/2855/J
* 9 7 8 1 9 4 1 9 0 7 5 6 6 *